I

Ecstasy
© 2010 Bella Andre

Chapter One

Luke gave Claire one of his trademark smoldering glances, the kind that kept her and her vibrator company when she was alone in bed at night, dreaming of him. After ten years of platonic friendship, after a painful decade of hearing about every woman who had passed in and out of Luke's bed, Claire knew it was time for things to change.

Maybe her new confidence came from the three Manhattans she'd already gulped down. Maybe it was because they were celebrating her promotion to Senior Vice President of SF BankCorp, and she was giddy with her new found power. Whatever the reason, Claire simply didn't care about anything else tonight, outside of the promise she read in Luke's eyes.

Uncrossing her long, supple legs, and then re-crossing them slowly for impact, she scooted to the edge of her bar stool and leaned in close to Luke in the steamy bar. Keeping her eyes trained on his mouth, she found the courage hiding deep within herself and said, "If I have to look at your lips for one more second without tasting them, I think I'm going to go crazy."

Luke's eyes didn't widen in surprise. And he didn't make things any easier for her by leaning in to kiss her. Instead he raised an eyebrow, puckered his delicious lips slightly in a half-smile, and said, "Prove it."

The heat between Claire's legs increased several degrees and her nipples grew hard beneath her sexy silk top. For once in her life it was time to feel, not think.

Leaning forward until she was so close she could feel his breath on her lips, she reached up with her thumb and gently stroked Luke's bottom lip. A shiver ran through her, and she felt as if her nipples were going to break through the fine silk of her top.

She wondered if anyone else in the bar had noticed how incredibly turned on she was, but she forced the thought aside. She wasn't going to ruin her one chance at seducing the only man she'd ever loved because of what some strangers thought.

She had imagined feeling his lips on her breasts so many times, just touching them with her fingers was almost enough to make her spontaneously come in her seat. His lips were almost rough to the touch, and she wanted to explore every square millimeter of skin, from the corner where his upper and lower lips met so exquisitely, to the incredibly sexy, yet masculine bow in the middle of his upper lip.

Part of her wanted to go as slow as possible, to savor the sensations already washing through her in waves. But the other part of her, the part that made her pussy lips drenched and hot, wanted nothing more than to straddle Luke, right then and there at the bar, to sink down on his cock one inch at a time until she was on the edge of the best orgasm of her life.

Lighter than a feather, Luke darted his tongue against her thumb. Claire groaned, practically in pain, her need for him was so great. Grasping her wrist with his strong, warm hands, he held the fleshy part of her palm up to his mouth and nipped at her sensitive skin.

Claire was shaking now and hornier than she'd ever been. Her pussy was soaked, all without one single kiss. Then again, just thinking of Luke had always been enough to bring her right to the brink.

She was so caught up in her need, she barely heard Luke whisper, "Taste me."

Trying to break out of her fog, she moved to

obey his command as quickly as she could. Closing the distance between them, taking his breath as her own, she licked at the middle of his lower lip with the tip of her tongue, the same place she had already memorized with her thumb.

"What flavor am I?" Luke asked her, again so softly she could barely make out his words.

"I need another sample," she said, and captured his incredible mouth in hers, tasting every inch of him, relishing in the feel of his tongue against hers.

In her wildest dreams, she never knew a kiss could be so hot. She'd give up her vibrator forever for a lifetime supply of his kisses. Lord knew, if he kept it up, she was going to be moaning so loud everyone in the bar would be forced to stop their conversations to watch the live sex show happening right in front of them.

Luke pulled away from her and threw a $20 bill on the bar. Grabbing her hand, he pulled her off the seat and dragged her through the teeming crowd. Her skin was so inflamed, every time her breasts rubbed up against some stranger she had to bite her lip to keep from crying out. In the back of her mind, she wondered if she should be embarrassed that she was feeling so incredibly sexual.

No*, she told herself.* I'm going to take tonight as far as it can go. Tomorrow I'll go back to being the straight-laced banker the world thinks I am. Tonight, I'm a sex goddess!

Luke got them out the front door in record time and into the balmy summer night. Within seconds damp air made Clare's silk top cling to her like second skin. Luke promptly directed them down the nearest alley, nearly running in his haste.

Claire was breathing hard, but not from their quick pace. She knew what was about to happen, and on the verge of every single one of her dreams coming true, she was working hard not to hyperventilate in fervent expectation.

Turning down another alley, this one even darker and narrower than the first, Luke stopped abruptly and pushed her against the cool brick wall. Reaching his hands under her shirt, he cupped her full, high breasts and squeezed her nipples while he leaned his head down to devour the pulse of her neck with his mouth and teeth.

"Luke," she moaned, wrapping one of her long legs around him, trying to pull him in closer to her. "I can't wait another second."

He reached down to her short skirt and pulled the hem up to her hips. "You're not wearing any panties," he growled into her mouth, consuming her lips once again as he slid two fingers inside of her. "You're so wet," he said reverently against her lips, the bulge in his pants growing even more huge against her thigh.

Claire ground her hips into his hand and began to cry out as an orgasm ripped through her. Luke covered her mouth with his, taking in her scream, muting it with his tongue.

As wave after wave coursed through her,
Luke unzipped his pants and pulled out his cock.
Wrapping her hand around it, he said, "Guide me
into you. Now."

Claire's eyes widened. She always suspected
he was big, but even in her wildest imaginings she
couldn't have come up with this. His cock had to be
at least ten inches long and two inches in diameter.
What if she couldn't take all of him?

Luke must have sensed her reluctance,
because he said, "Don't worry, baby. You're so wet
I'm going to slide right in."

Grabbing her ass with his hands, he added,
"Wrap your legs around me."

Doing just that, suspended in mid-air, she
positioned the tip of his cock between her thighs.
Wanting to remember the sensation of his cock
entering her for the first time, she slid his head
around on her lips, on her clit, until he was
drenched with her juices. She could tell he wanted
to plunge himself into her as hard and fast as he
could, and she admired his restraint and the way he
let her pace their lovemaking.

Slowly, painstakingly, Claire slid the first
inch of him into her, and as she stretched to
accommodate his cock, she felt herself on the verge
of another orgasm. Right there on the edge, she slid
in another inch while Luke held her up against the
wall, poised on his cock as if she weighed no more
than a fly.

Unable to wait another second, she let

*gravity pull her down onto the last eight inches.
Nothing had ever felt so good to her in her whole
life and she fell into the second biggest orgasm
she'd ever had as Luke squeezed her ass cheeks
while lifting her up and down, sliding his cock in
and out of her.*

*Pulling his head back to look deep into her
eyes, he said, "I've always loved you," and then
pumped into her, all the way to the hilt, rocking
back and forth rapidly as he shot his seed deep
within her. Claire went straight from two orgasms
into three, even as her heart filled with the deepest
joy she'd ever known.*

Charlie saved his file and rubbed the tired
muscles on the back of his neck with his hands.
"Too bad real life can't be like my books," he
muttered, trying to remember when the last time
was he'd actually had sex.

"Ancient history," he grunted as he got up to
take a shower. He had another blind date tonight,
but he didn't have any higher hopes for this one
than the multitude of other dates he'd been on in the
past five years.

In fact, he wouldn't be surprised if all of the
single women in San Francisco had been spreading
the word about him, to warn each other off, in a
show of female solidarity.

He let the scalding stream of water pulsate
against his chest as he tried to shake off his
depression. "She's out there. She's got to be." His

words reverberated against the tiled shower walls. Drying off and dressing quickly in chinos and a polo shirt, he slipped on his watch and grabbed his wallet and car keys.

Right on time he pulled up to the café and was pleased when he saw the cute blond sitting alone in a booth by the window. Getting out of his car, he walked up to her and held out his hand in greeting.

"Hi. I'm Charlie. Are you Sophie?"

The blond nodded happily. "I sure am," she drawled in a light Texas accent.

They ordered white wine and chatted as they sipped their drinks, beginning the process of getting to know each other better. Charlie could tell that Sophie liked what she'd seen so far. She wasn't so bad herself, and he hoped that she would be more open-minded than the last thirty or forty women he'd dated.

"So," she asked coyly, "what do you do all day? Your friend Bob didn't tell me much about your line of work. Is it something top secret?" she asked hopefully, all the while eyeing the platinum band of his watch, taking in the expensive label on his shirt, and the faded leather of his $500 Italian loafers.

Charlie smiled engagingly. "I'm a writer."

"Ooohhh," she said. "How exciting. What do you write? Mysteries? Action?"

"Actually," he said, striving for a confident tone, "I write erotica."

The silence was deafening. Not bothering to hide her sneer, his blind date said, "You're a porno writer?"

Charlie cleared his throat. "No, I write sensual romance. Women make up 99% of my audience. It's really quite…"

But before he could get another word out, his date stood up, said "You pervert!" and splashed her entire glass of ice water on his face. Then she grabbed her purse and stomped out on her four-inch heels, her tight little ass wiggling in outrage all the way down the street.

Charlie wiped the shards of ice off of his face and chest, while the waitstaff openly laughed at him.

"That's a first," he muttered to himself as he stood up and headed for his car.

Usually his blind dates were satisfied with looking scandalized and making excuses about getting home early because the babysitter called with an emergency. At the very least, he had to give Sophie points for originality.

But no matter how he tried to frame the situation, he was sure of one thing: he wasn't getting any closer to finding the woman of his dreams.

Chapter Two

Evan laid Sara against the silk sheets and stood back to admire the way the firelight danced off of her creamy skin. She was the sweetest girl in the world, and he'd been waiting years for this moment.

Sara's cheeks were rosy and she nervously licked her pink, delicious mouth. "Are you going to take your clothes off too?" she asked him innocently.

Evan smiled and kneeled at the side of the bed between her legs. He didn't want to frighten her any more than she already was, but he was having a hell of a time trying to rein in his passion.

It pleased him immeasurably to know that Sara was a virgin, and that she had been saving herself for him, for their wedding night. He had waited so long for this night, for her to finally grow up. Of course, even though he had spent the past several years walking away from their chaste kisses and straight into cold showers, he had been with his fair share of women. But he always knew, no matter how good the sex was with these other women, he was simply releasing pent-up steam and honing his *skills for the one woman who really mattered.*

"I am, sweetheart," he said, stroking her hand lightly with his own. "But first I want you to experience deep pleasure."

"Oh, I have Evan. Your kisses are incredible," she sighed, trying to sit up so that she could kiss him again.

Getting up onto one knee, he leaned towards her and captured her mouth in a passionate, scintillating kiss. "Kissing is only the beginning," he said, promise in his eyes.

Sara opened her mouth into a darling "o" and blushed prettily. "Should I be doing anything?" she asked hesitantly, and Evan was touched by how much she wanted to please him.

"Oh my darling," he said, pushing his hands into her silky blond hair. "Just lay back against those pillows and I'll do the rest." Kissing her again lightly, he said, "And remember, there's nothing to be afraid of, because I love you and this is how I want to show you my love."

Sara followed his instructions and lay back against the pillows. He ran kisses down her neck and got caught up in worshiping her breasts.

He marveled at the sensual picture she presented. Her nipples were rosy and had formed into tight buds as he neared them. Even the swell of her breasts had a delicate pink flush, proving that she was as aroused as he was.

Cupping her breasts gently in his large hands, Evan ran his thumbs over her taut nipples and blew warm air across them. Sara gasped and he bent down to rain soft kisses all over the soft, sweet flesh, making sure he stayed away from the place she needed him to touch most. It wasn't until she was writhing on the bed in torment that he took pity on her and slowly took one nipple into his mouth, swirling the nub with his tongue, tasting her on his lips.

At that moment, Sara arched her back into him, pushing her breast even more deeply into his mouth. He nearly lost control of himself, more ready than ever to rip his clothes off and mount her like a stallion. Pulling from a deeper well of control than he knew he possessed, he continued to give loving attention onto her other breast, making her moan with pleasure.

Moving lower, he nipped and kissed her flushed skin across her tight belly, while running his hands up and down her quivering thighs.

His attention was soon wholly focused on the soft, wet mound before him.

Her blond, curly pubic hair was wet with her juices, and her scent was intoxicating. He ran his open hand down her stomach. Lightly, he slid his finger between her lips and then slowly into her.

"Evan," she moaned, her head thrashing back and forth on the bed.

"Oh baby," he said, his voice thick with lust and emotion. "You have the sweetest pussy."

He saw her eyes widen and slipped his finger back out, and stood up partway to kiss her again.

"You're so beautiful. Am I making you feel good?"

Blushing again, Sara replied, "I've never felt like this before. Is it normal?"

Evan laughed softly and brushed the hair out of her eyes. "What we have is amazing, baby. Trust me and I'll take you all the way to heaven."

Sara swallowed, and then said, "I do trust you."

Laying her back down, he knelt between her legs again. This time, he couldn't help himself, and he leaned in and tasted her wetness with his tongue.

She nearly bucked off of the bed, and he held her thighs firmly with his hands to keep her pussy right where he wanted it.

He plunged his tongue into her several times before focusing on her swollen clitoris. Taking it into his mouth, he swirled his tongue around once, slowly. Then, taking the utmost care, he swirled it again. At a snail's pace, he teased her clit, savoring every moment of his fantasy becoming real.

Sara grabbed his head to push his face down harder into her mound and he knew she was on the verge of coming. He abruptly changed tactics and flicked her clit rapidly and firmly until she was crying out with joy, her spasms taking over her body for a long while.

Evan stood to remove his clothes as quickly as possible. He was greatly pleased when Sara pushed herself up into sitting position and began to rip off his clothes in haste. But once they had pulled off his slacks together and were taking off his boxers, she stilled.

Looking up at him, she said, "I'm afraid, Evan."

Cupping her face in his hands, kissing her thoroughly, getting her used to her own sweet taste, he said, "I promise you, it will only hurt the first time. Only until you get used to having me inside of you."

Sara nodded and slowly reached for the waistband of his boxers, pulling them down his hips with excruciating slowness. When his shaft sprang free she gasped.

"You're so huge!" she exclaimed.

Evan chuckled softly, thrilled that she was so impressed with his cock. "And I'm all yours," he said as he took her small, soft hand in his and wrapped it around his shaft.

"Mmmm," Sara said. "You're hot too." She ran her hand up and down his length, getting used to the feel of him.

But Evan couldn't take any more teasing, so he gently pushed her back into the silk sheets and leaned over her, careful not to put too much of his weight onto her. Placing the head of his cock between her pussy lips, he gently probed her wetness.

The way Sara was writhing underneath him made him want to ram into her without waiting even one more second, but he wanted her first time to be perfect, so he governed his lust. Pushing in no more than an inch, then two, he heard her swift intake of breath and felt the barrier that guarded her most precious gift.

Poised above her, gazing deeply into her eyes, he said, "I never want to hurt you again," and then forced himself to push past her barrier, until he was practically touching her womb.

She cried out softly in pain, but within moments he knew her virgin's muscles had adjusted to the feel of him as she began to rock her hips back and forth in an age-old rhythm of love.

Her body eagerly swallowed his cock and Evan lost all control, pumping hard and fast into her. Beneath him, Sara met every thrust and together they cried out in a magical simultaneous orgasm.

For Evan and Sara, their wedding night was the beginning of a lifetime of love, better than anything they could have ever conjured up in their dreams.

Candace finished reading the final words of her chapter and looked up at the faces of her new writing group expectantly. The silence was heavy in the library meeting room. She couldn't miss the shocked expressions on the faces of her fellow writers.

Several people cleared their throats, and to get the ball rolling Candace said, "I'd love to get some feedback on the ending of my story. I just wrote it yesterday, so it feels pretty fresh to me."

Sixty long, painful seconds ticked by before one of the older ladies spoke up. "Candace, I'm not sure about the, ahem, appropriateness of the passage you just read us."

"The appropriateness? It's erotica. I'd say a sex scene is pretty appropriate." She searched the eyes of the other members of the group for some support, but found none.

Exasperated, she said, "I thought I made myself very clear with all of you before joining this group. I write erotica. Explicit romantic fiction. That means there's sex in it. And you all said you were okay with it."

Right as a man and woman excused themselves from the room, a forty-ish man spoke up. "I thought it was an excellent passage, Candace. You perfectly captured your hero's deep feelings for the heroine."

"Thank you," Candace said, flashing a smile at him, but before she could feel better about her evening, an old biddy who had just contributed a story about her cat said, "I will not stand for such smut! I think we should take a vote right now. Who here wants to listen to this trashy porn?"

Only the middle-aged man half-raised his hand, giving Candace a sheepish grin, and she had the awful feeling that he was only voting for her because he thought she was easy.

Looking smug, the ringleader asked, "And

who wants her to leave immediately?"

Everyone else raised their hands while their eyes shot daggers at her.

"Fine," Candace said, calmly slipping her papers back into her leather satchel. Swinging it up onto her shoulder she stood and left the room without a backwards glance.

She was none too surprised when she heard footsteps behind her in the hallway and turned to see her one supporter hurrying to catch up with her.

"Candace," he said, slightly out of breath. "I feel terrible about this."

"I'm sure you do," she said, a slight twinge of bitterness lacing her words.

"Even though this didn't work out, I was hoping that, ah, maybe I could take you out for dinner next Saturday."

Candace acted like she was considering his words carefully. Forcing a coy look onto her face she asked, "Is that all you want from me?"

Giving her a sleazy smile, he leaned in until she could smell his bad breath, and said, "I'm game for helping you try out some of your new scenes, any time you want."

Candace worked hard to keep her hands firmly at her sides. He wasn't the first guy she'd wanted to slap, and he wouldn't be the last. From between gritted teeth she said, "I don't know why every guy who meets me thinks all I want to do is fuck his brains out simply because I write erotica. Because I wouldn't have sex with you if you were the last man on earth."

Clearly upset by her slam, he looked her up and down and disdainfully said, "Then maybe you should stop begging for it, you slut," then ran back down the hall to the meeting room, slamming the door behind him.

Standing in the hallway, stunned by her latest bad experience, Candace heard the distinct sounds of lovemaking coming from the women's bathroom. A minute later, the two people who had left the room right after she read her chapter emerged, clothes in slight disarray, and sneaked back off towards the meeting room, thinking no one was the wiser.

Candace smiled momentarily. "I guess that means it was a good chapter," she said. But then, falling despondent again over the difficulties of her new writing direction, she added, "At least some people are having a good night."

Trying not to be too down about the events of the evening, she headed out for her car and another lonely night curled up on her couch with a paperback, where she could dream about having a perfect life, like the characters in her favorite books.

Chapter Three

Candace stood underneath the huge "Sensual Writer's Conference" banner and took a deep breath. As soon as she walked through the double glass doors she would officially be entering into her new life. Instead of continuing to write young adult stories, where sex was never allowed to enter into the storyline, today she was officially going to make the jump into the world of erotica, where the only limit was how far a writer wanted to go. Practically nothing was forbidden.

Now, if she could just muster up the nerve to walk through those damn double doors.

She tried not to be too hard on herself. After all, anytime anyone made a career change they were bound to have some butterflies in their stomach. Unfortunately, what Candace was feeling went far beyond butterflies. More like huge ravens flying around inside of her, picking at her innards.

A middle-aged woman brushed past her and hurried inside the conference hall. Candace knew it was now or never—time to either bite the bullet and commit to doing the work she loved, or to wimp out by continuing to write the same old stories she'd been pumping out since college.

"If she can do it, I can do it," Candace told herself firmly. She squared her shoulders, fluffed up her orange curls with one hand and set off for the door.

Candace was so focused on her goal, on making it past the threshold of her current comfort level, she didn't see the attractive, muscular man who was just about to step through the doorway. They collided as Candace bumped into him in a particularly graceless way, the full-body impact knocking them both to the floor. Candace tried to catch her breath as she lay in a heap atop the stranger.

Absolutely mortified by her clumsiness, Candace scrambled to get up off the man, but not before she became aware of the firm muscles of his butt, back and shoulders rippling beneath her.

Overcome by both embarrassment and a rare jolt of lust, she blathered on and on without being able to stop herself. "Oh! I'm so sorry! I can't believe I didn't see you and then I walked right into you and then I fell onto you and now we're on the ground and are you okay?"

Pushing himself up on his palms and then spinning around so that he was sitting on the cement floor, the stranger gave her a devastating smile. Brushing the dust off of his slacks, he stood up and said, "I'm just fine, thanks."

Candace was bowled over by the dimple in

his left cheek and could do little else but gape.

"Besides," he added with a mischievous glint in his eyes, "who wouldn't want to have a gorgeous woman lying on top of him first thing in the morning?"

Candace felt her cheeks turn pink, and she covered them with her hands, hoping to cool them down.

Looking slightly repentant, he said, "I hope I haven't made you uncomfortable. I'm just joking around. You looked like you were heading into the Coliseum to face the lions."

Candace dropped her hands from her face and gave him a small smile. "I feel like such an idiot for knocking you over."

The blond hunk held up his hand to stop her from lambasting herself any further. "I can't stand to hear you insult yourself. Especially since I don't even know your name yet." Holding out his hand he said, "I'm Charlie."

As the warmth of his skin covered her cold hand, she relaxed for the first time since she'd parked her car that morning. "Candace. It's nice to meet you."

She could tell he was trying to put her at ease as he picked up her leather bag and handed it to her. "Is this your first conference? I've never seen you here before."

Candace nodded. "Is it that obvious that I'm a newbie?"

"Nope, that's not it. I'm just pretty sure if

I'd ever met you before, I'd have remembered."

Candace blushed again and silently admonished herself to cut it out. "I'm sort of new to this genre."

"To erotica, you mean?"

"I'm really excited about making the switch from young adult fiction to sensual romantic fiction, but I guess I'm feeling a little overwhelmed today by it all."

Charlie smiled. "I know exactly how you feel."

"You do? Are you new to erotica also?"

"Nope. I've been going at it," he stopped and cleared his throat. "What I mean is, I've been writing erotica for a little over five years now. I can honestly say it is the most enjoyable, challenging writing I've ever done. But when I first made the switch from crime to erotica, it was pretty daunting."

While he talked, Candace thought there was something vaguely familiar about Charlie, but she couldn't quite put her finger on it. In any case, although she was greatly enjoying talking with him, she was worried about monopolizing his time.

Rather briskly she said, "Thanks for the pep talk, Charlie. But I don't want you to feel like you have to baby-sit me all morning. I'm a big girl. I'll be all right."

Giving her an enigmatic look that set her heart pounding like a drum in her chest, Charlie brushed off her concerns.

"You know what, Candace?" he said, her name rolling off his tongue like warm butter. "I'd like nothing better than to show you around the conference hall and to introduce you to some of my friends and colleagues." Leaning in closer to her he added with a wink, "Not that I don't think you're capable of taking care of yourself, of course."

This time, instead of blushing at his double-entendre, Candace laughed. "Thank god I'm starting to get your sense of humor," she said. "And by the way, if you're going to be my chaperone, why don't you call me Candy? The only people who ever use my full name are either my mother or my elementary school teachers when I really got into trouble for something."

Clearly unable to stop teasing her, in a rough undertone Charlie asked, "Did you get into trouble a lot, Candy?"

Candace swallowed and stared into Charlie's deep blue eyes. The flash of lust she had felt when their bodies had collided was jumping inside of her full-force now. Forcing herself to remember to be cautious, to remember how badly she'd been hurt, a shadow passed over her eyes.

Shrugging, she finally replied, "More times that I can count."

If Charlie noticed her swift change of demeanor, he didn't let on. Looping his arm through hers, he said, "I'm going to take you in now. But I'm warning you to be prepared for lunacy. We're a naughty little bunch, you know, us erotica writers."

Shaking off her painful memories, Candy smiled up at Charlie. "Lead on, oh wise one," she said in mock subservience. "Lead on."

Charlie directed them into a crowded common room, which had at least a hundred different information booths set up inside. Candace gaped at the displays all around them and started to wonder if it was too late for her to make her escape.

Seeming to sense her growing embarrassment in that incredibly perceptive way of his, Charlie held firm to her hand. "Now just remember," he said, leaning down to whisper in her ear, "there's nothing to be embarrassed about with these folks. We're all in the business for the same reason—because we love it. No one's going to look down upon you or call you a pervert today, I promise."

Shivering as his breath gently blew against her ear, she looked up at him, a question in her eyes. "How did you know people have been giving me a hard time about writing erotica?"

Charlie gestured to the group of people in the room with them. "Every one of us has had to deal with misconceptions at one point or another." With a grimace he added, "And I'd be lying to you if I said it's all a bed of roses, even after five years."

Suddenly, Candace was overwhelmed by the clear picture of the two of them, entwined together on a bed of rose petals. As warm heat pooled between her legs, she forced the vision from her head.

Thankfully, he didn't wait for her response and led them up to the first booth by the door, which, to Candace's dismay had the most comprehensive display of dildos she had ever seen amassed in one place.

Actually, considering she had never even gotten up the nerve to walk into an adult bookstore, they were the only dildos she had ever seen outside of a magazine ad.

"Candy, this is Albert. He's an old-timer around here, and frankly, without him, none of us erotica writers would be worth a damn."

Candy managed to muster up a smile for the gray-haired, bearded man, and reached out her hand to shake his.

"Don't be shy, missy," he barked at her. "Feel free to wrap your hands around any one of these babies to find out what they really feel like. I've got rubber. I've got really life-like skin. I've got hard dildos and soft dildos and dildos with vibrators attached. They come in a range of colors, including day-glo green with florescent pink stripes, if you're really looking for something to spice up a scene."

Candace wanted nothing more than for the ground to open up and swallow her whole. She had never been so uncomfortable in her entire life. What made her think she could write erotica, she wondered frantically. For god's sake, she had never even been able to have an orgasm during sex. And she certainly had never used a vibrator, or any kind of penis-like dildo to get herself off. Considering how naughty she felt when she used the stream of water from her hand-held shower head to bring herself to orgasm, she now had to face just how far over her head she was.

"Albert is a walking guru of sex toys. Thank god he's willing to share his knowledge or I'd look like an idiot in more books than I'm willing to mention."

Candace nodded mutely, knowing words were beyond her at this point. Not letting her run off, Charlie held fast to her hand. "We'll talk to you again later Albert," he said as he directed them to another booth.

At first glance, this one looked to be far tamer than Albert's booth, with a simple display of hardcover books for sale. Candace breathed a sigh of relief.

Introducing her, Charlie said, "This is my friend Candy. Candy this is Steve Holt. He's pretty much a hero around here."

Laughing, Steve said, "Only second to you, buddy." Turning to greet Candace, he said, "Welcome to the wild and wacky world of erotica. Unbuckle your seat belt and enjoy the ride."

Candace laughed and gave silent thanks that everyone was working so hard to put her at ease. Of course, she knew that meant she was probably walking around with a panic-stricken look on her face.

And when she caught sight of the cover of

Steve's latest book, she almost gasped aloud. Depicted on the cover were two women in sixty-nine position along with the title, *Sixty-Nine Kinds of Love.*

Knowing she was trapped in a full-body flush, with Charlie's hand tucked in hers, all she could think about was what it would feel like if his head was buried between her legs, his tongue lapping at her clitoris. No matter how hard she tried to clear the sexy vision from her mind, she just couldn't.

Fortunately, the two men were busy catching up with each other, and hadn't noticed her reaction to the sexy book cover.

"So, how's the new book going Charlie?" Steve was asking him.

"Pretty good," Charlie replied, running his free hand through his golden blond hair. "I'm having some trouble with my character's motivations, but I'll figure it out in time."

Steve laughed and said to Candace, "I swear to God, this is the only author I know who wants to know what his characters ate for breakfast in high school. Most of us are content to be able to do a character sketch for their past couple of years."

"Wow," Candace said to Charlie. "You sound pretty thorough."

The look Charlie gave her was so hot she felt seared to the bone. At least to her panties, which were beginning to feel distinctly moist between her legs.

"I am," he said hoarsely and then blinked hard a couple of times.

Clearing his throat, Steve said, "Oh, I almost forgot. There's a woman here from the Chronicle and she wants to interview you about *Morning Dew.*"

Candace gasped. "You wrote *Morning Dew*? You're Charlie Gibson?"

A faint flush stole across his face. "That's me."

Too stunned to keep the words from falling out of her mouth, she said, "You're the reason I wanted to get into erotica."

Realizing her sentence had come out all wrong, she tried to backpedal, saying, "What I meant is that I absolutely love your books. They move me more than anything else I've read."

Charlie looked incredibly pleased. "Really?"

Cutting in, Steve said, "You're not the first person who became a convert after reading his stuff. At least half of the people in the room did the very same thing."

Suddenly, Candace felt incredibly foolish. "And here I am, taking up all of your time, when so many people must be dying to get a word with you."

Amazingly, Charlie refused to relinquish her hand.

An attractive, medically enhanced brunette, whose tits were each the size of Candace's head, sidled up to Charlie. "I was just over at the mentoring table and they told me you don't have anyone under you yet." Licking her lips for impact, having stressed the word 'under' as if it was a magical spell she could weave around him, she pouted and added, "They said you had the final word on who you were going to work with." Walking her long, polished nails up his arm she said, "So, are you free for some lessons?"

Candace wasn't sure if her mind was playing tricks on her, considering her gut was teeming with jealous bile, but she thought she saw Charlie flinch and back away from the silicone Amazon.

Turning to her, with a cunning smile on his face, he said, "Actually, Candy has already snatched me up."

"I did?" she said, before she caught the pleading look Charlie was pinning her with. Trying to recover from the shock of being singled out by the man she respected more than any other writer of erotica, she smiled and slapped him playfully on the arm with her free hand, trying to look like she was just joking around.

"Of course, I did. I'm just teasing you." Then she turned to the Amazon-bitch and said with false syrupiness, "Actually, I tackled him the minute I saw him walking through the doors to make sure he'd be all mine."

Glaring at them both with fire in her eyes, the Amazon spat out "Your loss," at Charlie and then went in search of new prey.

Charlie led Candace into a semi-private corner of the room. "I'm really sorry about that back there. If you don't want me to be your mentor, I understand perfectly."

Candace blinked in confusion. "I don't even know what my mentor is supposed to do."

Giving her a reassuring smile, Charlie said, "All of the established writers sign up to work with a new writer. You know, to show them the ropes."

Candace's brain was assailed with visions of Charlie tying her up to golden bedposts, while she writhed underneath him and begged him to fuck her as hard and fast as he could. She shook her head, wondering when the hell she had started to have such incredibly vivid sexual daydreams.

Looking up at him, suddenly shy, she said, "I can't think of anyone I'd rather work with."

And just like that, she leapt head first into the unknown, with the most sexually potent man she had ever encountered.

Chapter Four

Charlie paid the delivery boy from the *Love You With Flowers* floral design shop on Chestnut Street in the Marina and then watched him get back into his delivery truck and drive away. He picked up the surprisingly heavy cardboard box of red, pink, and purple rose petals, placed them on the floor of his foyer, and closed the front door with a soft click. He leaned his forehead against the back of his front door and closed his eyes.

At least a hundred times in the past week, ever since he had coerced Candace into letting him be her mentor, he had told himself not to fuck this up. From the first moment he met her, in the instant that she had landed atop him in the conference hall, he knew she was special.

Unfortunately, every time he thought about Candace he got lightheaded and his heart started beating to a heavy-metal rhythm within his chest.

He thought back to their phone call, the Monday after the erotic writer's conference and groaned, remembering how lame he sounded as he outlined his mentoring plan to her. He banged his forehead against the door several times as his words flooded back into his brain.

"Thanks so much for offering to work with me, Charlie," she'd said.

He'd said, "You know what? I think we're both going to get a lot out of this." But then as he realized how smarmy he sounded, he backpedaled. "What I mean is there's nothing more enlightening than trying to teach another person what you already know. It's a good chance for me to see if I actually know what I'm talking about, or if I've just been faking my way through my last eight books."

Belatedly, Charlie realized he was going on and on about utter nonsense so he added, "Does that make sense?"

His palms got slick and sweaty on the handset of his cordless phone as he waited for her response.

Clearly trying to put him at ease, she said, "I know exactly what you mean, Charlie. And by the way, I've been thinking we should probably be upfront about things."

"What things?" Charlie asked, so suddenly nervous his heart was going clackity-click and he could swear he heard a heavy metal soundtrack in his head.

"I want you to know that you don't need to worry about the vocabulary you use when we're talking about work. I know you're a complete gentleman and that everything we do during our lessons is purely professional." She cleared her

throat and then added, "Even if we do happen to
deal with things like dildos and kinky sex in our
books."

Charlie forced a chuckle, but inwardly he
felt like the world's biggest scum. Sure, his
intentions were honorable. He was going to teach
Candace how to write great erotica. But he couldn't
deny the fact that in the privacy of his imagination
he had already devised twenty different ways he
wanted to make Candace scream with pleasure.

But no matter how strongly he felt about
her, he had decided to put the lid on his desire until
their mentoring sessions were through—jumping
her bones during their lessons would be a complete
betrayal of her trust. He only hoped it didn't kill
him in the meantime.

"Good," he'd said. "I'm glad we are being
completely upfront about everything right from the
start. I knew you were the right person to work
with."

"Frankly, I was afraid that Sheba Queen of
the Sluts wouldn't have left you in one piece by the
time she was done with you. I had no choice but to
save you by offering up myself."

Charlie let himself savor the vision of
Candace tied and bound to an altar, naked and
gleaming, in sacrifice for him, before he said, "I
appreciate that. More than you know."

"So, what's on the agenda?" she asked him,
and just like that his entire body broke out in a
sweat as he unfolded the piece of paper he'd written

their lesson plan on.

Trying to keep his voice light, he said, "I've broken our mentoring sessions into five different lessons. Lesson one will be how to set a romantic scene."

"That sounds great. I love the way you paint pictures with words in your books."

"Thanks," he'd said, and then swallowed loudly as he prepared to continue spelling out his list of lessons. Lesson one was the easy one, and he knew things were only going to get harder from here. Especially if the rock-hard bulge in his pants was any indication.

"Let's see, for lesson two I thought we'd work on varying positions." He had to pause, clear his throat. "I mean, we'll take a look at...uh, you know study the different ways that..."

Suddenly he couldn't think of any way to rephrase the sentence that wouldn't sound like he planned on screwing her brains out the minute she walked through his door.

Thankfully, she reminded him in a gentle voice, "Charlie, you've got to stop worrying about offending me."

"Okay," he said, but his trepidation must have been clear in his voice, because she said, "Say fuck ten times to me."

"Huh?"

"Just say it," she demanded.

"Fuck, fuck, fuck, fuck, fuck, fuck, fuck, fuck, fuck, fuck."

"Good. Now say, 'I want to lick your juicy pussy.'"

Charlie choked on an intake of breath, but he did as she asked. He repeated, "I want to lick your juicy pussy." Even as he imagined how amazing she would taste, he braced himself for her disgust, expecting her to say, "You're scum and I never want to talk to you again."

"Feel better now?"

He took a moment to gauge his feelings and realized, much to his surprise, that his palms were dry again and his heart rate had returned to near-normal. Candace, in her sly way, had forced him over the hump of his anxieties. Yet again, he was impressed by what a clever little piece of work this delectable woman was.

"Thanks for that." He was glad to laugh. "You definitely have a knack for dialogue. And now that I've decided to stop being such an idiot, here are the rest of my lesson plans." He spoke quickly and didn't pause between lessons. "Lesson three – using toys. Lesson four – the joy of sex in exciting locations. Lesson five – how to use role playing to really up the ante."

He knew if he gave himself even a second to think about her reaction he'd start to make an even bigger ass of himself than he already had, so he barreled ahead. "So, how about we start next Saturday at my house on Lombard? Noon?"

"Great," she'd said and hung up as soon as he gave her his address.

Now here he was, on the big day, with noon quickly approaching. Through great force of will, Charlie stopped banging his head on the door, stopped torturing himself with thoughts of what a dweeb Candace must think he was, picked up the box of rose petals and walked into his guest bedroom to finish preparing the classroom.

Charlie had decided the best way to teach Candace how to set a romantic scene was to show her one in real life. He knew, however, that using his master bedroom for any of these lessons was a very bad idea. As it was, in the past seven days he had beaten off to the picture of her he had in his head so many times while lying in his bed and while showering, as soon as he walked into his master bedroom it was practically a reflex for him to reach for his cock and start pumping it in his hand.

Standing in the doorway of his large guest room, he surveyed the space with a critical eye. He had draped the four-poster queen-sized bed with Indian silk. In his writer's mind, he could see two lovers deep within their own world, sheathed in the exotic fabric.

He had covered the mattress in red plush velvet, and underneath the luxurious cover, he had put red satin sheets. To top it off, a dozen pillows fought for space near the head of the bed.

Charlie had never been particularly interested in interior design—although he felt that he had done a nice job with making his house a comfortable and cozy reflection of himself—but as he went from store to store in Union Square, as he ran his fingers lightly over the fabrics, he realized that he was, in fact, greatly enjoying himself.

His enjoyment, he thought ruefully, may have sprung from his intense desire to see Candace wrapped in the silks, velvets, and satins he purchased.

Or, more to the point, his even more intense desire to *unwrap* her.

He tried to shake the image of Candace naked with her legs spread wide open before him, begging for him to ram his cock inside her. He needed to focus on the task at hand.

He had draped the windows with shimmering translucent red fabric, shot through with gold thread. Then he'd brought light back into the room with candles of varying sizes and colors, which he had placed on every possible surface.

On the bare wood floor in front of the rock-framed fireplace he had laid a chenille rug. It felt so good to the touch in the store he couldn't resist buying it. If Candace lay face down on the rug and rubbed her breasts across it slowly, what would the soft fabric feel like brushing against her nipples?

The rose petals were the final touch. Checking his watch and noting it was a quarter to twelve, he bent down, opened the large box and reached into the mass of flower petals.

To his great satisfaction the scent of the roses wasn't overpowering. As he had hoped, the flowers lent an alluring air of sweetness to the room.

When the box was empty and rose petals beautifully littered the room, he started a fire in the fireplace and then painstakingly lit each of the candles. The room had a sensual vibe and fairly glowed with romance, just as he had hoped it would.

The doorbell rang, jolting him out of his pleasant trance. His palms went damp again and he half-laughed, half-groaned at how ridiculous he was being. All he and Candace were going to do was look at the bedroom, study its romantic elements, and then do a writing exercise using it as the setting for a story.

No big deal.

Charlie walked down the hall towards the front door and told himself to pretend he was working with Steve Holt. Why should he be nervous? They were just a couple of writers doing research for their craft.

He opened the door and all of his good intentions came crashing down upon him.

He instantly took in her smell, the pulse moving under the soft skin on her neck, the way the breeze was moving the tips of her red, curly hair around on the tops of her luscious breasts. An image of her pubic hair, red and curly and moist with her come and his saliva, popped into his head.

He was in deep, deep trouble.

By the time he remembered to say, "Hi, come on in," he had no idea how much time had gone by since he'd opened the door. Thirty seconds? Five minutes? Time was a blur.

How could he treat her like one of the guys when she was a walking, breathing orgasm waiting to happen?

* * * * *

Candace walked into Charlie's foyer and tried not to betray her nervousness by giggling, babbling, or checking to see if her hair was out of place. Instead, she plastered a big smile on her face and squeezed past Charlie and through his front door. He hadn't moved aside very much to let her into his house, but she had to admit she didn't mind rubbing up against him, not one bit.

He was just as gorgeous as he had been at the conference, with the highlights in his blond hair picking up the sunlight, that streamed in through the windows. She took in the snug fit of his well-worn jeans. She couldn't keep her eyes from straying to the light brown chest hair that peeked out through his long-sleeve shirt. Salivating at the thought of seeing his chest—which she knew she'd never get a glimpse of in this lifetime, but a girl could dream, couldn't she?—Candace wished he had left a couple more buttons undone.

Charlie's bare feet were the icing on the cake. Candace had never seen such sexy feet before. She had never even known feet could be sexy. Until now. His feet were tan, with well-manicured toenails and a light dusting of hair. Suddenly, she saw herself naked and ready for him, straddling his big toe and…

No! Candace stopped herself from taking her daydream any further. What was happening to her, she wondered, as she swallowed past her dry tongue. Everything she saw made her think about Charlie's cock and fingers and tongue.

Her mind was turning into an X-rated pay-per-view channel.

Trying to force her thoughts away from the incredibly dirty things she wanted to do to each and every part of Charlie's body, she tuned into the details of his house.

It was crazy, but Candace felt that Charlie was even more potent, even more intoxicating when he was within the walls of his private environment. His home, like the man himself, was masculine and yet warm all at the same time.

"So," she said in a bright voice to break the awkward silence, "this is your house, huh?"

As the words left her mouth, Candace turned pink and had to fight the urge to run out of his front door, down his steps and back into her car. Could she have sounded any more like an idiot?

Charlie's eyes seemed to refocus in on her and he said, "Yup. Sure is. Glad you could come."

"It was my pleasure."

He smiled at her and she melted under his gaze. She knew she had a serious case of hero worship, but this was worse than she had bargained for. *Don't make a pass at him under any circumstances*, she told herself in a firm inner voice. *He's your teacher, and you should be grateful that he is taking any time out of his busy and illustrious schedule for you*, she added with a flourish.

She noted he looked a little uncomfortable as he said, "I've set up a classroom of sorts for us. It's down the hall." But when he comfortably added, as if she were a buddy from his baseball league, "Let me pour you a glass of chardonnay," she decided his discomfort was just a figment of her imagination.

Her mind was playing tricks on her. More likely than not she was projecting her own uneasiness onto him.

She followed him into his kitchen. "You have a beautiful home."

He turned to smile at her as he uncorked a bottle of white wine. "Thanks. It's a big change from my last one."

"How so?"

Candace hoped her question didn't seem like she was prying, although she acknowledged that she definitely was. By the time their lessons were through, she wanted to know everything she possibly could about Charlie Gibson. She was already tucking all the little details of his clothes and his furnishings away into her memory for safekeeping and leisurely review on lonely nights. Who knew, she might even buy herself her own personal dildo if she was feeling really brave.

"I got to design this house from the ground up. And I, uh, didn't have anyone telling me she hated my ideas this time around."

He handed her the wine glass and said, "That's probably a whole heck of a lot more than you wanted to know, isn't it?"

She laughed and patted his hand. "Trust me, I know exactly how you feel."

But as she felt a tremor pass through her from simply touching his hand, she immediately pulled back and said, in a shakier voice than she intended, "Should we get started with things, Mr. Mentor?"

He nodded. "I've set things up in the guest room. Follow me."

She followed him out of the kitchen and down the hallway. When he opened the door to the guest bedroom she was overwhelmed with the sweet scent of roses. Her heart started to beat double time so she joked, "Are we going to write a story about the florist and—"

Her words stopped altogether as she rounded the corner and stepped fully into the room.

She gasped. "This is amazing!"

Candace wanted to rub herself on all of the luxurious fabrics draped across and above the bed. She wanted to feel the rug under her toes. She wanted to wrap herself in rose petals.

Turning to Charlie, she said, "Did you do all this for me? For our lesson? You shouldn't have gone to all the tr—"

He smiled at her and cut her protest off. "I really enjoyed creating this room. And now that I've seen the effects of if myself, I think I'm going to leave it as a nice surprise for my house guests. Although, I probably won't see much of them 'cause they'll be so busy going at each other."

Candace forced a laugh and started worrying in earnest as Charlie sat down on the chest at the foot of the bed and motioned for her to sit next to him.

"I think you need to take off your shoes and socks to fully appreciate this bedroom."

She knew he was right and she was certain that he wasn't the least bit interested in her, so she set her wine glass down on the mantle of the fireplace, then sat down next to him and removed her shoes and socks.

Playfully she said, "Should I take anything else off?"

Charlie's eyes got wide for a moment and then he grinned wolfishly. "I suppose you'd better, otherwise, how are you going to write about the feel of the material brushing across your heroine's skin?"

"Oh, do you really think I should?" Candace said, some panic creeping into her voice. But then, as she looked around the room at the candles and the fire and saw the velvet and silk beneath her, she decided, what the hell.

Not giving herself the chance to think, she pulled her v-neck sweater over her head, leaving only a skimpy tank top covering her torso.

"Okay," she said impishly, vowing to let herself be carried away by the mood for once in her life. "I'm undressed."

Charlie looked her up and down. "I'm not sure I'd call you undressed, but it's certainly a start."

Suddenly, something inside Candace clicked into place. Or broke down completely. She wasn't sure which. But the new voice inside her was loud and clear.

She spoke quickly, before she lost her courage. Before she came to her senses. "Charlie, you know how we agreed that everything that went on during on mentoring sessions was going to be strictly professional?"

"Yeah?" he said, drawing out the word as a question.

"Well, it has just occurred to me that it's one thing for me to appreciate this room as a writer." She paused and then said, "But it's another thing entirely for me to experience it as a woman."

She saw Charlie's Adam's apple move in his throat and clenched her hands into tight fists at her side. She didn't know how she was going to manage it exactly, but she wasn't going to be a wimp and back down. Not here. Not now.

For the first time in her life, Candace was going to go for what she wanted. She reached for the button on her jeans and Charlie's hand shot out to grab hers.

"What are you doing?"

She half-grinned at him, but she knew she was far too nervous for it to look like a smile. More like she was baring her teeth at him.

"I'm taking off my clothes."

He blinked at her in confusion. "Oh."

Candace tried not to let his utter non-reaction to the idea of her taking off her clothes bother her. She wasn't here because he thought she was a sexy woman. She was here to learn about the art of erotic writing. And if she had to do it on her own, by god, she was doing it.

She stood up and unzipped her pants. As she lowered them to the ground, she looked up at Charlie, who was still sitting in stunned silence on the edge of the chest.

"The fact is, I have never experienced the sensation of silk sliding against my skin. I've never lain naked in front of a roaring fire. I've never rubbed my nipples against satin." She looked at him imploringly. "These are all things that I have to do or I'll never be able to write about characters who know what these physical sensations feel like. Can you understand that?"

Charlie nodded.

She stood in front of him in her skimpy tank top, knowing her nipples were jutting out and she forced herself not to flinch, not to run, and not to cover up. She hooked her thumbs into the thin straps of her silk thong undies and said, in a soft but firm voice, "I won't pressure you into joining me,

Charlie. I'm sure this is all pretty old hat to you, but it's all brand new to me. So I could sure use some help if you were willing to instruct me." Lowering her eyelashes to cover her eyes, she licked her lips and then made eye contact with him again. "In a purely professional way, of course."

"Whatever happens inside the classroom stays in the classroom?" he asked in a calm, detached voice.

A little shiver worked itself up Candace's spine. Trying to sound as unaffected by her near-nakedness in an incredibly romantic room with the most potent man she'd ever met, she said, "You got it."

In the blink of an eye, Charlie replaced her hands with his on the sides of her thong.

With a new gleam in his eyes he pulled her closer to him, so that her muff was mere inches from his mouth.

"Let the lessons begin."

Chapter Five

Charlie hooked his thumbs under her panties and slowly pulled them down to her thighs. Her pussy was pink and so hot he could feel the heat emanating from it, practically scalding his face. Her auburn bush had been waxed and trimmed into a Brazilian style—mostly smooth and glistening skin with just the barest patch of hair in the middle. Her lips were plump and he was more glad than he could ever say that she had just given him permission to touch her, to taste her, to spread her legs wide open and plunge into her until he had quenched the sexual need that had ridden him hard from the moment he'd met her.

Pushing her panties down around her knees, he pushed her thighs apart and her lips separated slightly. He slipped the index finger on his right hand into her tight, dripping cunt a couple of inches. She moaned and wiggled her pussy against his finger, so he pushed it even further inside her until his palm was cupping her entire vulva and his thumb was covering her swollen clit.

He lifted his thumb and blew softly on the

swollen flesh. Her vagina clenched around his finger, and he wondered just how close she was to coming. He blew on her clit again and slid his finger in an out of her pussy. Just as he had suspected, she was a powder keg waiting to explode. Sensitive to each spasm of her slick yet powerful pussy muscles around his index finger, he bent his head down an inch or two and barely touched the tip of his tongue to her firm, throbbing flesh.

She pressed against him, begging for a tongue fuck. Grasping the back of his head with her hands, she ground his face into her pussy, crushing herself against his lips and teeth.

Charlie knew what she wanted, even as she thrashed onto him. Slipping his middle finger into her pussy to join his index finger, he continued to slide his fingers in and out of her in a slow, steady rhythm. He gripped her firm, round ass in his left hand and pointed his tongue so that all she felt against her clit was the hard tip. As if he were typing the same letter over and over on a typewriter, as if she was the page he was making his mark on, he moved his tongue steadily up and down on her clit as she cried out with pleasure.

Finally, the pulsing of her muscles around his fingers slowed and Candace's body went limp. The muscles in her back and butt cheeks tightened up as she tried to pull away from him, but he wouldn't allow it. She might not have known what she was getting into when she made her "let's get naked because we're professionals" comment just minutes earlier, but now, whether she liked it or not, he would decide when they were finished.

After all, he was the teacher.

And she was the very promising new student.

Quickly, he put his arms around her trim waist and threw her onto the plush bedding, face down. As her body hit velvet, it was as if flowers rained from the sky. Several rose petals landed on her ass, thighs, and calves. Charlie moved to straddle her on the bed, blowing each of the rose petals off one by one until all that remained before him was her naked, creamy skin. With every breath, Candace whimpered her pleasure.

She started squirming, but when she tried to turn around, he quickly moved to straddle her, leaning over her back to cup her full breasts in his hands through her tank top. He whispered in her ear, "I'm going to take off your shirt now so that you can feel the velvet rubbing against your nipples."

She stopped squirming and in a voice so quiet he could barely hear her she whispered, "Okay."

Charlie sat back up with a leg on each side of her thighs, the huge bulge in his Levis pressing into the curve of her ass. He grinned as he slid his fingers underneath the hem of her tank top.

He liked hearing her quick agreement, liked running the show.

After years of women making him feel like

he wasn't worth their time due to his choice of profession, after years of women using him only for his huge bank account, Charlie savored the sensation of being in complete control of a woman's body and soul.

Knowing he had already given her intense pleasure so quickly only served to up the ante.

Her breath quickened as he slowly rubbed his fingers underneath the hem of her shirt, along her rib cage. With infinite precision he dragged her cotton shirt up her ribs until it caught on her breasts, which were much larger than he had thought a week ago at the conference.

If someone had asked him to guess her cup size he would have confidently said she was a B-cup, given her small frame. But now, having held her globes in his hands, even only for a moment through her thin, damp cotton shirt, he knew himself for the fool he was.

Candace was definitely at D cup. At least.

Slipping his hands between the plush velvet coverlet and her shirt, he hooked his thumbs up under the hem of her shirt and tugged it up over her tits. As he pushed the shirt past her nipples and the tips of his fingers covered her tits, he heard her rapid intake of breath and almost came in his jeans. He was already breathing like he had run a marathon.

"Put your arms up," he whispered into her ear and as she obeyed him he slid the tank top off of her body and threw it to the floor.

Candace turned her head to face him, but he already had a plan of action and was not going to let her deter him. Putting his hands on her rib cage, he lifted her torso slightly off of the bed so that her nipples were just barely touching the velvet.

"I'm going to rub your tits against the cover and I want you to focus all of your attention on how good it feels."

She nodded, just barely, showing him she understood. He pressed his groin into her ass, which pressed her mound into the velvet. He separated her legs with one of his and her juices soaked through the denim covering his legs. Roughly, so she could feel the coarse fabric pull and tug against her tender lips, he moved his thigh up and down against her.

Tightening his hold on her ribcage, he lifted her torso up just high enough that her nipples floated just above the velvet cover. "Your breasts are the only thing in the world that matters, Candy. Forget about my thigh rubbing between you legs. Forget about how much you want to turn around wrap your legs around my waist."

She groaned and tried to protest, so he squeezed her ribs tighter in his strong hands.

"Do as I say," he said forcefully. "It's for your own good."

Candace's body tensed underneath him for a split second before her hips started to buck wildly against his leg. She was coming again, convulsing helplessly against his leg. His mouth curved up into a steamy look of satisfaction as he drove his thigh against her pussy and gave her what she wanted.

The fierce rocking of her lower body blew dozens of rose petals off of the bed, into the air and onto the floor.

The mingled scents of her pleasure and the rose petals were a fragrance he knew he would never be able to forget.

But he still hadn't forgotten his goal. Before they left the room, before lesson one had come to its incredible, unforgettable end, he wanted her to realize just how sensitive a woman's breasts were, so that she could write powerful sex scenes in her books that left no part of the female body unexplored.

He almost laughed aloud as he realized what a poor job he was doing of fooling himself that he cared one whit about her writing skills at this moment as he lay over her, his fingers mere inches from her tits, his leg practically jammed up inside her cunt.

They could offer him the fuckin' Pulitzer Prize right now and he wouldn't care. Frankly, what he was doing in his guest bedroom—what he and Candace were doing together—had nothing to do with writing and everything to do with sex. And he wanted Candace to experience sex in its most heightened form. With him.

Still holding her rib cage in his large hands, he began to slide her torso ever so slightly back and forth, so just the tips of her breasts were rubbing up against the velvet fabric on the bed. He thought about turning her over and taking her tits into his mouth and sucking them, nipping them until she was crying out again, and he barely kept his own needs reined in. But what kind of teacher would he be if he changed the lesson plan mid-way just because his cock was about to explode in his pants?

He heard her whimper again and he knew she had fallen ever so slightly back down to earth from her explosive orgasm, so he leaned forward and whispered again in her ear, "You're going to come again, sweetheart. Any minute now, you're going to feel the way the velvet caresses your rock-hard nipples. You're going to realize that your breasts are the center of everything."

She started to say, "Charlie, I," but he cut her off saying, "Shh. I don't want you to talk to me. I want you to feel."

He wrapped his left forearm around her waist, while still rocking her breasts gently side to side on the velvet comforter, and ran the fingers of his right hand down from the bottom of her rib cage, down along her flat stomach, which convulsed as he lightly touched her skin, to the top of her mound.

"Uh uh uh, Candy," he admonished her when she strained to move her clit closer to his finger. "What did I tell you?"

"My breasts," she gasped.

He smiled and moved his fingers down a millimeter. "That's right. If you keep doing what I want, I'll keep doing what you want."

A small sob left her throat, and he knew she was close, so close that if he so much as touched the tip of her clit with his fingertip she'd explode again in his hand. He moved his left arm slightly. He was still holding her torso suspended from the bed, but now every time he slid her body to the left side on the velvet her breast slipped into his palm.

"Charlie!" she moaned and again he had to fight the urge to rip his jeans off and split her wide open with his cock.

He kept his palm open at first, so that all she felt on her nipple was the callused skin of his open palm. "Are you focusing on your breasts and only your breasts right now?" he asked her in a low voice.

He saw her nod her head and rewarded her by moving his right hand another millimeter towards her clit. Even though he was no further than the top of her slit, her juices were soaking his hand, so he rubbed his fingers around in circles on the slick skin of her well-waxed mound.

As he slid her left breast into his palm again, he held her still and pinched her nipple between his fingers, rubbing it between his thumb and middle finger. At the same time he plunged his hand down into her wet, hot cunt and ground one finger and then two and then the tip of a third into her.

She screamed "Charlie!" and the muscles of her pussy clenched as they tried to hold his fingers hostage.

When she was still so far gone, still so

entranced by the waves of pleasure washing over her, he took advantage of her pliability and effortlessly rolled her over onto her back.

Looking at her luscious breasts for the first time, he gasped at her perfection, at her beauty in the candle-light, surrounded by the deep hues of the silk, satins, and velvet furnishings.

Her breasts were lush melons and he knew immediately that they were entirely real, with no silicone added. Having felt one of them in the palm of his hand, he knew how deliciously heavy they were. His mouth watered as he anticipated tasting them.

Don't get ahead of yourself, Charlie, he warned himself. He had to stay on track with his lesson plan. *All in good time,* he told himself. *All in good time*.

Candace's eyes were just starting to open and she was trying to refocus them on his face, when he slipped a length of richly patterned silk fabric off of the bedpost. He quickly grabbed her right wrist and tied one end of the cloth around it and the other end about the bedpost. He slid yet another length of fabric around her left wrist and tied that one up as well.

"You're such a good student we're moving straight to lesson two."

Her eyebrows scrunched down in an unspoken question as he splayed her legs and tied up both her ankles to the nearest bedpost.

"Varying positions is lesson two."

He tied the final bow on her left ankle, then gave into the losing battle, letting himself lap once at her very wet, well worked vagina, with his tongue.

She tried to buck up into his mouth, but he had tied her just tight enough that she couldn't move more than an inch or two off of the bed.

He took one of the thin pillows from the headboard and slid it underneath her perfect ass.

Breathing hard, he said in a low voice, "I just want to look at you for a few moments before we take this any further."

* * * * *

Candace's head was spinning. She had definitely surprised herself when she decided to take off her clothes during the lesson. But after coming three times in rapid succession with a virtual stranger, in his guest bedroom, during her mentoring session, she was more than surprised.

She was stupefied.

She was flabbergasted.

And damn it, she was still horny as hell. Hornier than she'd ever been her entire life. And this was how she felt after *three*, count 'em, *three*, mind-blowing, soul-shaking orgasms.

Candace could hardly believe it when the first "Big O" had rocked through her. During a decade of lackluster sex, she had never, ever had an orgasm with a man in the room. She couldn't believe how quickly she responded to the barest touch from Charlie's tongue, from his finger inside her swollen labia.

And then again with his muscular thigh between her legs.

And then again with one of his hands on her breasts and one between her legs.

Oh god, she thought to herself, *he must think I am a total slut. Just like that other woman with the huge fake tits who wanted him to be her mentor.*

She looked down at herself and realized he had tied her to his bed. *I'm no better than that bitch from the conference. And now he knows.* But worse than having her hero know what a slut she was, was that *she* now knew what a slut she was.

Suddenly wanting to be as far away from her embarrassment as possible, far away from Charlie's probing fingers, from his tongue and his all-seeing, all-knowing eyes, she laughed nervously and said, "Charlie, I feel like I'm all spread out for you like you're Jesus and I'm The Last Supper."

He was still kneeling between her legs, clothed in his Levis and light blue striped shirt, and she could see where her come had stained the fabric near his wrists and along his right thigh.

She was so embarrassed she wanted to die. *Right here, right now, God, you can take me. Please!* What she didn't add to her plea, although she wanted to, was, *Now that I've experienced pleasure like this, it's all right for me to go. At least,*

I know I've truly lived in this man's arms.

He didn't laugh at her lame joke about the Last Supper. Instead he leaned over and lapped at her pussy once more. She felt all of the remaining blood from her head and the rest of her body rush between her legs, straight to her clit. If she weren't so damn embarrassed, she would have begged him to lick her just a couple more times.

One more touch and she'd be over the edge into oblivion.

For the fourth time in the past hour.

She was Candace Whitman, for god's sake. A girl who had gone to Catholic school with ruler-thwapping nuns. A girl who still turned bright red every time she thought about the astonishing array of dildos on display at the erotic writer's conference.

But before she could make any more feeble protests about how ridiculous it was for him to have her splayed open and tied up like some sort of sex slave on his four-poster bed, surrounded by rose petals and a hundred candles, Charlie slid another length of silk fabric off the four-poster bed frame. Slowly, as if he knew how much his every move tortured her inflamed libido, he twisted the thin fabric into a tight cord.

Then he stood up and began to walk around the side of the bed. She wondered, somewhat wildly —hopefully too, much to her ongoing chagrin over what an utter and complete slut she was turning out to be—if he was going to whip her with the tip of the fabric. She knew it would hurt. But then, she knew Charlie would make it feel good too. And then he could kiss it all better.

Instead, he took the fabric and covered her eyes with it, lifting her head slightly so that he could tie the fabric in a knot behind her head.

Candace had never felt more powerless.

And she had never been so full of anticipation in her whole life.

Firmly tamping down on the logical part of her brain that said their lesson had gone too far, way too far, she let her senses take over. She listened to the crackling fire, the sound of Charlie's footsteps on the wood floor and then the carpet. She smelled the potent scent of rose petals mixed with her own come and the faint scent of vanilla from the candles. She tasted her own musky desire on her lips.

Feeling silk slide around her ankles and wrists, holding her hostage, for the second time in her life, for the second time in one short, sunny afternoon, Candace gave herself up to a greater power.

The power of truly sweet lovemaking.

And wondered why she had never let herself experience it before.

Chapter Six

Charlie had watched the play of emotions work their way across Candace's face as he'd turned her over on her back. Feelings of self-doubt and self-consciousness were the reasons why he had wanted her face down for his initial onslaught. It was so much easier for her to let herself go if she forgot anyone was watching.

From what she had already said to him, from all of the nervous signs she tried to conceal from him, he knew how badly Candace wanted to experience incredible heights of lust and passion. He knew she wanted to learn what it was to fuck and be fucked so hard and so long that the tender, slick skin between her legs was raw from it. And to still want more, even when pain was beginning to get all mixed up in the pleasure.

Knowing she was a beginner in the sensual arts, he was going as slow as he could with her. Putting her face down. Showing her how strongly she could react to the simplest, lightest touch. Letting her hide from her embarrassment. He wondered who had taught her that sex was dirty, but knew it was a conversation they would have later, down the line, when she had accepted what her body wanted from her.

Oddly enough, while Charlie was no sexual novice—he'd had his fair share of hot one night stands and had been sandwiched between more than one woman during the past five years since his divorce—he had never wanted to make love to anyone this badly.

Ever.

Not even when he was a fourteen-year-old virgin used to beating off to Playboy, and was finally ready to sink himself into the pussy of one his mother's friends who had come on to him, did he feel this out of control. It was taking every ounce of restraint within him, and then some, to keep from thrusting into Candace.

At the same time, he had never wanted to give anyone as much pleasure as he wanted to give Candace. He felt like he could make her come a hundred times and then a hundred more, and though his cock would surely be turning blue by then, he would gladly give up his own sexual release just to see her achieve hers.

Without knowing just how or when it had happened—was it the minute she walked through his door, or was it when they spoke on the phone, or maybe it was when she had accidentally tackled him at the conference—the teacher had become the student.

Charlie would have been amused by this

realization were it not for how painfully she aroused him. She was innocent, she was confused, she was unknowledgeable, yet her body had the answers from all the way back to Eve.

But they weren't done with her lessons yet and he knew the only way to keep her imprisoned in her own sexuality, the only way to show her how many ways she could feel good, was to take control away from her. So he tied her up and blindfolded her, praying all the while that he was doing the right thing. Hoping that he wasn't pushing her too far.

As he tied the knot around the back of her head and felt her soft red hair caressing the backs of his arms, he noted with satisfaction that the tension was leaving her body, almost as if she had made the decision to give in to everything he was offering her.

He stood and picked up one of the candles from the dark-pine bedside table.

"I want you to tell me if I'm hurting you, Candy," he said.

She swallowed once, then twice, then licked her lips, nodding her agreement.

He blew out the candle and then kneeled at the side of the bed. With infinite precision he poised the candle over one of her thighs and tilted it so that the barest amount of hot wax dripped onto her skin.

Candace hissed out a stream of air between her teeth as the wax made contact with her skin.

Immediately concerned, Charlie covered the patch of skin with his hand and said, "Did I hurt you?" If he had, he knew he would never forgive himself.

"No," she whispered. Her voice sounded heavy. Drugged.

Charlie breathed out an enormous sigh of relief, but he couldn't help but worry that he had crossed a dangerous line.

Instead she surprised him. "Do it again," she whispered.

His heart flip-flopped in his chest and swelled with something he couldn't quite name. He replaced his hand with his lips as he kissed her softly on her thigh, right above the now-dry vanilla wax. Reaching for another candle, he blew out the flame and slowly dripped a trail of hot wax up the inside of her left thigh, enjoying the sound of her moaning as the wax came closer still to her wet, hot pussy, enjoying watching her try, futilely, to move her sopping mound closer to his hand.

Again he followed the line of quickly drying wax with his tongue and his teeth as he nipped at her skin.

"Charlie, Charlie, Charlie," she whimpered with every touch of his lips to her skin, and Charlie wondered what the hell he was doing still fully clothed while a sex goddess was tied to his bed.

He reached for another candle and told himself to chill out. There would be time enough for him to pump into her wet, tight hole, but not before he gave her more of what she so desperately needed.

So he dripped wax along her stomach, and kissed his way along her rib cage, until his face was so close to her breasts he couldn't hold off any longer.

When he gently touched the tip of his tongue to one of her nipples, she nearly broke the silk binds off of her wrists.

"More!" she urged him. "Please!" she begged him.

Obeying her wishes, he took her nipple into his mouth and sucked her areola in as well. He wanted to be gentle, but he was too far gone himself to hold anything back. In the back of his mind he hoped he didn't bruise her, but he knew she wouldn't care even if he did, because she was moaning, "Yes! Just like that! Yes!"

As if he had a timer in his head, Charlie knew her fourth orgasm was long past due. And if he played his cards right, he thought he could move her from four to five in rapid succession.

Laving his tongue back and forth over the hard nub of her nipple, he moved his index finger into the cleft of her pussy and just as he touched her incredibly swollen clit he bit down slightly on her left nipple.

She screamed again and Charlie sucked as hard as he could on her breast while ramming his finger in and out of her feverishly.

Thinking of all the heat pooling in her juicy cunt gave Charlie an idea. He took the long, slim pillar candle and slid it into her, just a little at a time. By the sound of her moans, he knew she was still coming, and easily turned on enough for whatever he wanted to slip between her legs

In the midst of her orgasm, Charlie removed his lips from her breast and joined the candle with his tongue on her clit. Even as she was resurfacing from her explosion, he felt her twitching again beneath his tongue. He could feel the candle jerk as her inner muscles clenched.

Charlie untied the silk bindings around her arms and legs. Leaving the blindfold on, he picked her up in his arms. Her body was completely limp from her five intense detonations and slick with a faint sheen of sweat.

Gently, he carried her over to the chenille rug in front of the fire.

She wrapped her slim arms around his neck and as she sank into the deep rug, softly pressed her lips to his.

Charlie was unprepared for their first kiss, and even the merest touch of her lips on his was more than he could handle. Roughly he pulled the silk fabric away from her eyes and stood up, pulling off his jeans and shirt as he did so.

In a few seconds he was completely naked and kneeling on the rug between Candace's legs. He paused briefly, knowing it was longer than he could stand to wait, but he'd kill himself later if he didn't have this image of Candace burned into his brain forever.

He memorized every gleaming, creamy,

perfect inch of her incredible body, her luscious breasts. He pushed her legs open wide, bent her knees so that she could take him into her and reached for one of the condoms he had placed at random in the room, just in case he should get as incredibly lucky as he was right now.

Her eyes followed his movement, and she shook her head.

"No. I want you like this." She reached out tentatively to touch him with the tips of her fingers. "I want to feel you inside of me. Skin to skin."

Charlie wanted it too, more than anything in the whole world, but he was torn.

"I haven't been with anyone in over a year. So you don't have to worry about me."

He shook his head and grinned ruefully, "Me either."

"Thank god!" she exclaimed, laughing as she reached for him. As their lips touched, her laughter died in her throat.

"Take me, Charlie. I need to feel you inside me."

Her words were punctuated by a firm squeeze of her fist on his throbbing shaft. For a moment, he was afraid he was going to spurt all over the creamy skin of her belly.

Charlie reared up, kneeling between her legs. He wanted to watch as his cock slid into her pussy, just like the candle, but this time it would be his own throbbing flesh and blood pumping into her.

He angled the tip of his cock into her soaked labia and probed her entry with the very top of his head. The head of his cock was slick with his sperm, slick with his intense desire to blow inside her womb.

If she was going to come again, he wanted her to do it before he got inside her, lest the convulsing of her muscles send him to his own end too fast.

Reaching his hands up to her breasts, he rolled her nipples between his fingers, cupping her breasts. His cock was his weapon of delight on her pussy, her clit, and within moments her eyes drifted shut and her neck arched. Her hands held fast onto his ass as she came against him.

Taking a deep breath, he slid into her an inch. She was so tight, which he already knew from how snugly she held onto his fingers when he pushed them inside of her, he wondered how he was going to make it one more inch, let alone the next eight.

He grasped for control, not wanting to blow his wad before he had sheathed his entire shaft inside her. More than he had ever wanted anything his whole life, he wanted to feel Candace's slick heat wrap around his cock, her tight muscles milking him dry.

Gritting his teeth, he moved hands underneath her hips to cup her butt cheeks in his hands, and he slid in another couple of inches. She began to buck into him while using her own strength to pull his cock into her.

"Charlie, you feel so good," she moaned.

Charlie began to say, "Candy, you've got to let me move slow here. Or else..." but let his words drift off as she smiled a wicked little smile.

She lay back against the rug, rubbing her hands up and down his thighs. "I wouldn't want to disobey the teacher," she said, her voice a husky whisper of need. "You might have to bend me over your knee so that you can spank me," she added, her voice thick with desire.

A vision of himself spanking Candace's sweet ass as she cried out on his lap gave him no choice but to plunge as deeply as he could go. Mindless with the need to ravage her, to blow his seed as deep within her as he possibly could, he dragged her legs over his shoulders and rammed into her again and again.

Joined to him in the most elemental way, Candace's hips bucked wildly, taking him all the way inside, then forcing him back out along her slick canal. She cried out his name, begging him to send her over the edge, but the roaring in his ears was so loud, he could hardly make out her words. He thought he tasted blood in his mouth, figured he must have bitten his tongue in his crazy rush to savage her.

Breaking through his fog, he heard Candace's impassioned sob, "Oh Charlie, oh god, yes, yes, there, now!"

Gripping her hips against his, they pounded

back and forth in perfect rhythm. And as he
collapsed beside her, with his heartbeat sounding
louder than a bass drum in his ears, he said,
"Sweetheart, you are definitely an A+ student."

Chapter Seven

Sunday morning, less than twenty-four hours after the most mind-blowing sex of her life, Candace sat in her cozy home office at her cherry wood desk with her laptop open to a blank word processing file. She stared blindly at the cursor as it blinked at her.

"What happened to me yesterday?" she asked herself for the hundredth time. Her breath fogged up her computer screen, but she didn't notice. She couldn't see anything beyond the images in her head of her writhing beneath Charlie, of Charlie plunging into her, of his fingers wet with her, touching her, making her scream out his name again and again.

She couldn't for life of her figure out how she had managed to put her clothes on, find her way to the front door, get in her car and drive home. Less than twenty-four hours later, she looked back on the entire experience and could barely make out the details of the scene through the thick sensual haze that blanketed her memories.

It was as if she was looking into a forbidden

realm of pleasure, where only the privileged, where only the elite were allowed to participate. And since Candace knew she had never been one of those elite, her brain was bewildered by the entire experience.

She had hardly slept the night before. Every time she closed her eyes she could swear she felt the imprint of Charlie's tongue between her legs, and when she gingerly touched herself she was wet. So wet that she couldn't resist touching herself some more. She couldn't resist thinking about everything he had done to her body. Everything he had done that made her feel so damn good.

As soon as Sunday morning had arrived, bright and shiny through her windows, she dragged herself out of bed. She put on her robe, made herself a hot cup of strong coffee and sat down at her desk.

Candace had never let another human being control her before. Always, even when she thought she was in love, she held a part of herself back. Kept a part of her soul safe.

But with Charlie, surrounded by rose petals, candles, and sumptuous fabrics, she had given in to his every touch. If he had stopped touching her, stopped tasting her at any point, she would have begged him for more.

Disbelieving still, she shook her head and tried to make sense of her feelings. After she caught her last boyfriend cheating on her, after he had made it perfectly clear that it was her fault for being a prude, for being cold and lifeless in bed, she accepted that she was never going to know true passion. Even worse, she believed she wasn't good enough for the bastard and all the men who had come before him. They all wanted to fuck her boobs, but didn't give a shit about her heart.

But now that Charlie had pleasured her more ways in one afternoon than she had ever felt in the first twenty-eight years of her life, she wondered if it was because they had a deeper connection than just bodies.

She sighed and told herself to get over it. Just because their mentoring lessons had spiraled way out of control—Candace hadn't forgotten that it was entirely her own idea to take off her clothes —he was probably thinking how she was just another fan, another wannabe writer who wanted to get into his pants.

"I'm not in love," she said aloud. "I'm in lust. Big difference."

Feeling a little better, a little saner, Candace took a sip of java. Suddenly words began to dance through her mind.

Jolene was a good girl. She was the kind of girl boys took home to their mother's and said, "I'm going to marry her, Mom." They took one look at her angelic blue eyes and smooth golden hair and knew she was pure as driven snow.

Jolene had spent her entire life with nuns. In Catholic school uniforms. When she was a little girl, she thought every other little girl got ready to go to school in the exact same way she did, automatically reaching into their closet for the blue and white plaid jumper and white cotton shirt. She thought the only clothes in the world were white cotton knee socks and black patent leather Mary Janes.

Mary, Jolene's mother, was pleased with how well-behaved her daughter was. They were more like sisters than mother and daughter, and Mary thought Jolene told her everything. But if Jolene ever had secret thoughts in her pink and white ruffled bedroom late at night, under the covers with a flashlight, reading the latest Nancy Drew mystery about a mysterious boy who kidnapped her and gave her forbidden kisses, she never told her mother about them.

The day Jolene turned twenty-one, she was offered a full-time position playing piano for the church. For the first time in her life she was torn. She loved the nuns with all of her heart. Growing up in the safe environment of her private school had brought her nothing but happiness, but lately she had begun to feel a yearning inside of her that grew stronger every day.

Unbeknownst to her teachers, to her parents, and to her few chaste and respectful boyfriends, Jolene had been sneaking off to the used bookstore downtown and spending her allowance on books.

Jolene had long ago outgrown Nancy Drew. Her fingers trembled as she read Judy Blume. And then Jude Deveraux. And then Katherine Woodiwiss.

Jolene would have sworn that no one liked sex, that her parents had copulated only to create her and then settled back in their separate bedrooms as soon as her father's sperm sunk into her mother's egg.

In these books she saw a far different reality and knew it was something she had to experience for herself. Before she agreed to marry one of the boys who wanted her only as a wife and mother. Before she agreed to spend the rest of her days playing piano in accompaniment for little girls as they sang their hymns.

Bravely she told her parents and the nuns that she was going to spend some time in the city. She told them she was going to work with a local church there—which in fact she was, part time— and they were all so proud of her. Her parents found her an apartment and paid for six months' rent and didn't worry about their precious daughter. Why would they, when she had never given them even the slightest bit of trouble?

Jolene Mackenzie was a good girl.

* * *

Zane stood behind the bar and wiped another glass dry, sliding it beneath the counter in preparation for opening the bar. His bar.

He still couldn't believe "Piano Man" was

his. Every time he pulled up underneath the neon sign on his Harley, he got a rush. But as he wiped down the brass counter one more time, he frowned at his reflection. If he didn't find a great piano player, and fast, "Piano Man" would be a laughingstock among piano bars. Unfortunately, the last five guys he had auditioned stunk.

Hell, he could play better than them, and he could barely read a note.

Someone from outside pushed the door open slightly and a shaft of blinding light hit Zane across the forehead.

"Excuse me," he heard a timid little voice say.

"We're closed," he said gruffly. "Come back at five."

But the girl disobeyed him and walked through the door.

Zane looked at her in disbelief. The last time he'd seen someone as prim and proper as the young girl standing before him, he was in church looking at a nun. And lord knew he hadn't set foot in a church for well over a decade. Maybe two.

On second thought, no nun ever had such gorgeous blue eyes and a mouth he could imagine wrapped around his dick.

"I said we're closed," he said, glaring at her. It was pissing him off the way his dick was perking up just because some meek, blond girl, barely out of pigtails, was walking across the floor toward him.

"Are you the owner?" she asked him, as if she hadn't heard him tell her to leave twice already.

He glared at her, trying to scare her away, but when she kept staring at him with her huge, blue eyes, and held her ground, he nodded.

"What's it to you?"

She held up the want ads. "I'm here to apply for the piano job."

He snorted. "You?" He threw his head back and laughed in her face to drive the point home. "Honey, this ain't no church, and you certainly ain't no piano man."

Her face set in a mulish expression. She turned away from him, but instead of walking back out the door, she walked towards the small stage and sat down at the piano.

"I'm auditioning," she said, and he knew she was trying to be brave, but even in the dim light of the bar he could see her hands shaking.

He looked down at his jeans and cursed the huge bulge in the front of his pants before taking several menacing steps towards her. But before he could forcibly grab her by her skinny little shoulders and throw her out onto the sidewalk, she opened the Blue Book of Jazz and Pop standards and began to play.

He stopped in his tracks. She played thirty seconds of one song and then flipped the page and played thirty seconds of the next. Zane sank down into the nearest chair.

The little choir girl was incredible. The

piano player of his dreams. Shit! He couldn't have her in the bar. Every man in the place was going to start having dreams about laying her sweet little body over the front of his thighs, pulling up her pleated skirt and...

"Stop!" Zane said loudly, almost more to himself than to her, but this time she obeyed him.

"I want the job, sir," she said in a calm but firm voice.

"No. The bar is called Piano Man, not Piano Woman."

"That's sexual discrimination," she pointed out.

He rolled his eyes. "You're not good enough."

Her eyes shot fire at him. "Yes I am!"

Suddenly Zane had a thought. "How badly do you want this job?"

She lowered her long eyelashes and then looked back up at him. "I want it."

Slowly, Zane got up from the chair and sauntered over to her. Sitting down next to her on the piano bench, he said, "I'm willing to make you a deal." He saw her swallow and then she licked her lips.

"I'm listening," she said as she removed her slender fingers from the keyboard and clasped them primly in her lap.

He bent his head over hers until their lips were touching and then he slipped his tongue into her mouth, dying to taste her.

"This is what I want. Are you willing to give it to me?"

Her eyes grew even wider, but she nodded.
"Whenever I want?"
She nodded again.
"However I want?"
This time she smiled at him and reached out her hand to shake on the agreement. "I'm Jolene," she said in a voice as sweet as honey. "What's your name?"

* * *

That first night, Jolene played the piano like she had never played it before. She knew she was still on shaky ground. Besides, she was so excited and nervous about the terms of her contract with Zane, she needed to blow off her energy at the keyboard or she'd go crazy.

All night she had watched him out of the corner of her eye. In her fantasies, she had never created any man as incredible as this one. Six feet tall, and all muscle beneath his worn jeans and tight black t-shirt, his teeth gleamed white against the dark tan of his skin. Stubble covered his jaw line and his shoulder-length dark brown hair and piercing green eyes made him look so much like a pirate that Jolene felt as if he was living in the wrong century, on the wrong continent even.

At the end of the evening as the last customer walked out, he locked the door and then joined her on the stage again.

"Stand up," he said as he sat down on the piano bench.

She did as he asked and tried to get her knees to stop shaking. Pulling her so that she was standing between his knees, he reached around the back of her skirt and popped open the top button, then slid the zipper down until her skirt fell into a heap at her heels.

She looked around the bar at the hundred tea-light candles glowing, at the fireplace roaring, and knew that all of her fantasies were about to be made real.

He hooked his fingers into the edges of her cotton panties and slowly slid them off, over her ass and down her smooth, untouched thighs. Jolene had to fight the urge to cover herself from him, and she barely managed to keep her hands clenched at her sides.

Before she knew it he had moved his hand between her legs and slipped the index finger of his right hand into her vagina. She gasped even as she felt her muscles convulse around his thick, long finger.

Jolene was scared. She had barely even touched herself there in the shower. But she was so excited her fear hardly seemed to matter. She strained against his finger and he pushed it so far inside her his palm covered her and his thumb was pressing on the sensitive flesh at the top of her vagina.

She knew from her books that it was called the clitoris, but she could hardly think the word to herself.

"Your clit is so swollen," he murmured, his mouth less than an inch from the cleft between her legs.

She liked the way clit sounded coming from Zane's mouth and she forced herself to say the word out loud. "My clit has been swollen all night," she murmured.

He groaned, then lifted his thumb off her clit and blew softly on the engorged flesh. Her vagina clenched around his finger and as he blew on her again and slid his finger in and out of her vagina, she closed her eyes and started to see a rainbow of colors. Her legs were shaking uncontrollably now, but not from fear. She was trying to crest the tallest hill she had ever encountered, and she needed Zane to help her over it.

She put her hands on the back of his head and pressed his mouth to her. "Thank god," she cried as he worked his tongue and his teeth over her inflamed flesh and clasped her buttocks with his strong hands.

Jolene's world exploded in a blaze of fireworks. Now that she knew what awaited her on the other side, she knew she would never be able to go back to the perfect world she had come from.

Jolene Mackenzie wasn't a good girl anymore.

Candace looked up from her computer screen and realized she had been writing all morning. She reread the beginning of her new story and smiled.

Evidently, Charlie's lessons had inspired more than her underutilized libido. His incredible lessons had stimulated her mind and imagination as well.

But as she remembered their promise to each other to keep whatever happened in Charlie's "classroom" inside the classroom, she was assailed by guilt.

A bad little voice inside Candace's head said, *Don't worry, honey. He'll never read your book. He'll never find out that you and he are the live action figures playing out your sex scenes.*

Candace had never written so fluidly before. What's more, she had never been so inspired to continue with her story, to find out what was going to happen with Jolene and Zane.

I can't stop now. The words reverberated in her skull, so she said them aloud, announcing them to herself in her empty office. "I can't stop now. I *won't* stop now!" she proclaimed and gave up trying to win the battle to be the good girl she was supposed to be.

"Being good has always been my problem," she muttered, thinking how very close to the truth her new heroine Jolene was. And then Candace smiled again thinking about all the different ways Jolene was going to be bad, and couldn't wait to get the story finished.

Candace spent the rest of the afternoon typing away at her laptop computer, working hard to get every nuance and every emotion of her first two lessons with Charlie just right on the page.

And as she did so, Candace began to forget that she had ever lived a life without pleasure.

Chapter Eight

Charlie stood up from his desk and walked into the guest bedroom of his house. He hadn't been able to work since Saturday, since the day his whole life had been turned upside down by a redheaded vixen who didn't even know the power she wielded. He needed to call her, but as it was, he was still too chicken to dial her entire number without hanging up.

He hoped she would still talk to him. After the way they had parted on Saturday, after she stood up, put her clothes on mechanically, and then turned to him with a plastered smile and shook his hand, saying "Thank you very much for the lessons, Charlie," he wasn't sure if he had done the right thing with her at all.

His conscience was bothering him more than he wanted to admit. Above and beyond the fact that he was worrying he might have taken advantage of her, was the indisputable truth that if he were with her again, he knew he wouldn't have one single qualm about making her scream his name out, over and over again.

He was still upset that she had left after only seven orgasms, when he had planned to give her at least ten. He supposed, somewhat ruefully, the three times he took care of himself that night after she had left practically made up the difference. Nonetheless, he would rather have Candace coming in his arms or on the tip of his tongue, than his hand and his memory making him shoot all over the shower walls.

The phone rang and Charlie picked up the cordless handset on his shiny black and white kitchen island.

"Charlie Gibson."

"Hi Charlie. It's Candace. How are you?"

Charlie nearly dropped the phone he was so surprised by her phone call. "Um, uh, I'm fine. Great. Super." He thwacked his forehead with the back of his hand for sounding like such an idiot. "How are you doing?"

He heard her laugh across the wireless phone line and the choking sensation around his heart eased up a bit.

"I'm great Charlie. Really, really great. I wanted to thank you for your excellent lessons on Saturday."

"You do?" he asked and then tried to cover his gaffe by saying, "What I mean to say is, I wasn't sure if—"

Thankfully Candace cut him off before he could make an even bigger ass of himself. "I loved every second of it, Charlie. And you know what,

I've been writing better than ever."

"That's great," he said to her, and meant it. He hadn't written worth a shit since Saturday, but he didn't care at all. All he wanted was to see her again, but he was afraid he'd be coming on too strong, that he'd be too obviously sniffing after her if he suggested moving onto lesson three.

"Anyway," she said, "I was wondering if you'd be up for lesson three?"

Her matter of fact, professional tone confused him, again. Didn't she know what was bound to happen again when they got in a room together? But he was so glad she wanted to see him again, he pushed the thought aside.

"I certainly am," he said, trying to sound as detached as she did.

"Should we meet at your house again? Or mine perhaps?"

"Actually, this time I was thinking we would meet at a restaurant."

"A restaurant?" she said, her misgivings sounding clearly in her voice. "To learn about sex toys?"

He chuckled softly into the phone. "Don't you trust your mentor, Candace?"

She was silent across the line for a couple of seconds and he knew she was thinking it over. *Say yes,* his brain urged her telepathically.

"Yes I do, Charlie," she said.

"Great," he said. "Do you know where Oceanview Restaurant is on the edge of Golden

Gate Park?"

* * * * *

Candace was shocked by Charlie's suggestion. She had been shocked ever since she and Charlie had hung up that morning.

When she had boldly called him, she was completely sure she was going to have no problem rolling with whatever Charlie was going to throw at her. She couldn't suppress a shiver of delight as she imagined him using a dildo, or something even more creative, on her during this lesson.

She couldn't help the flicker of disappointment when it didn't look like that was going to happen. There was no way he could ply her with a dildo in a restaurant, was there?

Besides, wasn't learning about having sex in new locations lesson four, not lesson three?

She checked her makeup and outfit one last time before stepping out of the car. The previous Saturday at his house, he had seen her under forgiving candlelight and fire glow. As the sun hadn't set yet and he was going to see her in full daylight, she wanted him to think she was pretty.

She had dressed a little more risqué tonight than she usually would have for a date. She shook her head. *This is not a date*, she reminded herself again. He was her mentor and she was his apprentice.

If she read anything more into it than

professional education, she was going to end up with a broken heart. Candace figured she already had enough of those as it was.

Nonetheless, she had dug out a gold-sequined tank top from the bottom drawer of her dresser and paired it with a flirty black skirt, which brushed the tops of her kneecaps when she walked. She had swept her ginger curls up onto the top of her head with a gold clip and wore small gold-hoop earrings on her lobes. The final touch to her outfit was a pair of frivolous spike-heeled black and gold sandals that she had never had the nerve to wear before.

She left the parking lot and walked up the pathway to the beach. Charlie was waiting for her on the steps to the sand, looking out to the Pacific Ocean. She noticed he had a plastic shopping bag in his hand and shivered, wondering what was inside of it.

She put her hand on his arm and he turned around to face her with a huge smile on his gorgeous face.

"Candy," he said, "You look amazing."

She blushed. "Thank you. So do you."

He looked better than ever, which was really quite a feat considering how incredible he had looked the two other times she had been with him. He had dressed up slightly, wearing navy blue light-wool slacks and a pink pin-striped long-sleeved Ralph Lauren shirt.

He slipped her hand into his and was

moving towards the front door of the restaurant. She pulled back slightly, saying "I'm curious about what you've got in the plastic bag."

Charlie turned and smiled at her. "I was going to wait to give it to you until we went inside, but now's as good a time as any, I suppose." He opened the bag so that she could look into it.

"A pair of panties?" she said and looked up at him in confusion.

He nodded. "I want you to put them on."

"Now?"

"Once we get inside, go to the restroom and change out of the panties you're wearing."

Candace felt her face turn red. "And then what?"

He shrugged. "And then we'll eat and enjoy each other's company." He handed her the bag, then pulled her back up the steps towards the restaurant.

"Let's go inside. I'm starved," he said, and she had no other choice but to follow him.

Candace wondered how it was possible for her pussy to already be soaking wet when all she had done was say a few sentences to the guy. He was turning her into a walking orgasm, for god's sake.

They stepped into the foyer of the beautiful restaurant and he whispered in her ear, "I think the bathroom is just down the hall to the left."

A shiver ran down her spine – not fear, but anticipation - as his breath stroked her cheek and she obediently headed off to the ladies room, plastic bag in hand.

Once in a stall, she took a deep breath and wondered if she should cut bait and run before she got in any deeper than she could handle.

But then she thought about the hundred pages she had already written of her new book and how well it was going, and she knew that a true professional should be willing to give everything to her work, to try anything if it had the potential of enhancing her art. So after listening carefully to make sure no one else was in the bathroom, she slid her red silk panties off of her bare legs, folded them neatly, and slid them into her gold hand-purse. Gingerly opening the plastic bag, she pulled out a black thong.

"Is this it?" she whispered to herself in the bathroom stall, as she turned it this way and that, poking her hand back into the bag to see if there was something else.

Wondering what the big deal was about the thong, and knowing it was bound to be something good if Charlie was behind it, with her heart racing, Candace slipped her feet into the thong. Settling the panties up on her hips she let her skirt fall back down over her hips to her knees.

Wadding up the plastic bag into a ball, she stuffed it into the garbage can in her stall and stepped back out under the fluorescent lighting above the sink. Taking one last look at herself in the mirror, she thought she looked pretty confident considering how jumpy she felt. She grabbed her purse from the counter in front of the mirror and pushed the bathroom door open.

She rounded the corner and headed back into the entryway, careful to walk slowly so she wouldn't trip in her very high heels and make a fool of herself. She looked up and saw Charlie watching her carefully and she gave him a little grin. He reached into his right pocket and suddenly, she felt tingles, pulses between her legs.

She stopped dead in her tracks, propped herself up against the wall with her left hand and closed her eyes, trying to determine what had just happened to her.

She felt as if she had just sat down on a vibrator! Not that she would know firsthand what that would feel like, since she didn't own any self-stimulants, but she couldn't disregard the quivering sensation between her legs.

Comprehension dawned on her and she opened her eyes to meet Charlie's gaze.

He looked like a lion who had just captured a milk truck.

He held his hand out to her as he met her halfway down the hallway and said, "Good. I'm glad you did what I asked you to do. Now let's go eat."

"Eat?" Candace asked him, her voice squeaky, off its normal pitch. "We're really going to eat?"

The next thing she knew, the hostess was seating them at a table by the window, and Charlie was ordering drinks for them.

"This is a joke, right?" she asked him, half-hoping he'd say, *Yes, go put your regular panties on and then we'll head back to my place so I can fuck your brains out*, but mostly hoping he'd press the button on his little remote control again to send her into orbit.

"There are a lot of strangers in the room with us, aren't there?" he said rather wickedly.

Her mouth fell open. She quickly moved to shut it, intent on keeping her cool even though this third lesson of theirs was already moving far beyond their last lesson, far beyond her realm of comfort, far beyond anything she ever thought to encounter in her lifetime.

And here I thought I had experienced everything with him on Saturday, she mused silently as she pretended to study the menu. The words were a blur, and when the waiter came to take their order she couldn't seem to open her mouth. Thankfully, Charlie ordered for them both.

Candace was on pins and needles as she waited for the next surge of energy on her pussy lips, as she waited for Charlie to gratify and simultaneously embarrass her across the table. She was already incredibly wet, just from seeing Charlie, from the one jolt he had already given her, and from the sensual promise she read in his eyes.

"So, how was the rest of your day?" he asked her innocently, as if he didn't hold the control to her entire world in the pocket of his wool slacks.

She opened her mouth to reply, but her mouth was as dry as her pussy was wet. She reached for her water glass and as she lifted the cool rim to her lips, Charlie put his weapon of pleasure to use again.

The sensations that washed through her were so intense she nearly dropped her glass. Suavely, Charlie reached for the glass and slid it from her fingers back to the table without spilling a drop. She gripped the edge of the table and rode the waves of pleasure her panties were giving her under her skirt.

Charlie let off his cunt controller—as she was beginning to think of it now that she knew the absolute power he wielded over her—a second later when the waiter dropped off two glasses of champagne and two small salads.

Candace looked around at the other diners in the posh restaurant and wondered if any of them had noticed her writhing in her seat. From the expressions on their faces, she didn't think anyone had, thank god.

Charlie speared a crisp slice of tomato and held it out for her across the table. "Taste this," he said, and she noted he was holding the fork with his left hand, so she shook her head.

"No thank you," she said as formally as she could under the circumstances.

He took his right hand out of his pocket and put it on the table. "Look, both hands are free now." He held out the tomato slice again. "I want to watch your teeth and lips take in this plump, juicy tomato," he urged her and this time she acquiesced.

But as she began to open her mouth to slide the sweet fruit off of his fork, the buzzing on her clit began in earnest. This time, she was too close to the edge to fight off the explosion.

A low sound came from her throat, and she clenched the edge of the table so tightly the skin on her knuckles turned white.

"Let it go," Charlie implored her softly across the table.

Candace closed her eyes and let the waves of intense pleasure suck her into the abyss once again. Little whimpers escaped from her mouth, no matter how hard she tried to hold them back. She was dimly aware of Charlie's intent gaze as he watched her come.

Just as her orgasm had rocked all the way through her, turning her completely inside-out, their waiter approached their table with a concerned look on his face.

"Is everything all right here?"

Charlie let off the controls and looked expectantly at her, waiting for her answer. She smiled tremulously at the waiter and said, "Yes. Thank you. Everything's fine," hoping he would just get the hell away from the table and leave them alone.

Instead the waiter said, much to her ongoing chagrin, "It's just the look on your face while you were eating was—"

Their young waiter seemed stuck on searching for just the right word to describe the public agony of her sexual release, so she jumped in and said, "The tomato was *so incredibly good.*" She hoped her performance was a believable one.

Finally, he smiled at her and bowed a little, saying, "Good. Great. Your main courses should be out in just a few minutes," before he walked away.

"You really are an A+ student," Charlie said as she touched at the corners of her mouth with her napkin.

She couldn't decide if she was furious with him or falling harder for him than ever before. She decided to keep things light until she decided.

"And you are quite the inventive teacher, aren't you?"

He raised an eyebrow and slid the small remote control across the table.

She looked at him in surprise. "Why are you giving this to me?"

He reached for it again, saying, "I'm happy take it back if you want," but she grabbed it a split second before he did.

"No. I think it's better if I've got this with me for the rest of the meal." She slid the remote control onto her lap and put it underneath her napkin.

He laughed and ate a bite of his salad, washing it down with a sip of champagne before saying, "When I tell you to, I want you to press the on button."

"Are you crazy?"

It was one thing for him to drive her wild in public, but it was unthinkable for her to do the very same thing to herself!

He stared deeply into her eyes, his pupils slightly dilated, his breathing heavy and slow.

"Now."

She stared back at him, willing herself to stay strong, to stick to the only sense of herself she had even known, and shook her head once.

"I said now," he repeated in a clear, firm voice.

"No," she said as her heart raced straight to her throat and got stuck there.

"I'm only going to say it one more time," he said, his voice and face devoid of all expression. "Push the button right now."

And this time, she knew she had no choice but to obey him, although she wondered what delicious way he would punish her if she disobeyed him. In any case, she didn't have the strength for disobedience. Considering she was on the verge of coming just from the sound of his voice, she figured she may as well go for the whole damn thing. For that matter, she didn't want to look too deeply into the fact that her finger had been trembling over the on button ever since she slipped it beneath her napkin.

She took a deep breath that quickly turned shallow, pressed the button and turned the machine in her panties on. As she did so, Charlie said in too low a voice for anyone but her to hear, "I want you to keep your eyes open. Look at me while you're coming. And keep holding down that button no matter what else happens."

Candace felt hot, slick liquid pool between her legs as she digested his words. She trained her eyes on him, and every time she was tempted to shut him out, to experience this radical pleasure all by herself, he said, "Open up, Candy. Open up."

She lifted her heavy lids and instinctively widened her legs underneath the table, opening everything up for the man she was falling for heedlessly.

Candace was on the brink of bursting when the waiter arrived with their dishes. She was tempted to turn off the machine purring away on her clit, she began to lift her finger off the button, but Charlie's eyes held her in some sort of magnetic pull, so she continued to hold the switch down.

As she continued to detonate in her seat, the waiter set down their plates and then since they were obviously ignoring him, he stepped away from the table again without a word.

Charlie whispered, "You're so beautiful," and it was enough to make her close her eyes and fall back into her chair, holding onto the remote for dear life as she fell deeper and deeper into the void.

When she finally resurfaced, it took her several long moments to figure out what had happened, to remember where she was. All she knew was that Charlie was with her, as he had been for every one of the best sexual releases she had ever experienced.

She took in his broad grin across the table, and the expectant, slightly nervous look on his face suddenly made her want to shout out with happiness.

"Wow," Charlie said. "That was more intense than I thought it would be." He looked a little worried as he said, "Are you angry with me?"

"Nope," she said matter of factly. "It was a great lesson. At least as good as one and two." Taking a sip of champagne she leaned closer to him across the table and said, "I have to tell you, I can't wait to find out what you have planned for lesson four."

The look of surprise on Charlie's face turned into laughter and he relaxed back into his chair.

"You certainly are full of surprises," he said with obvious appreciation.

Candace just smiled a new I'm-All-Woman-So-Watch-Out smile. She waved the waiter over to their table.

"Could you pack up our food into a doggy bag and leave it up at the front desk?" she asked him sweetly. "We just remembered a meeting we need to be at right away." Reaching into her purse, she threw a wad of twenty-dollar bills onto the table and stood up.

She held out her hand to Charlie. "Come with me," she said in a husky voice.

He rearranged the enormous bulge in his

trousers and slid the chair back to stand up. Candace folded her small hand into his large, warm one and a shiver ran up her spine.

She was being so naughty! She hardly recognized herself as the woman she'd been for the past twenty-eight years.

Stepping outside into the ocean breeze, laughter bubbled up through her. Kicking off her shoes, she pulled Charlie along towards the grove of trees several hundred yards from the restaurant. They walked in silence until they reached the small forest.

Candace ducked her head to get under the branches of the nearest cypress tree and stepped inside to find a small clearing of soft, white sand in the middle of the circle of huge trees.

She turned to Charlie, who had followed her into the center of the grove, and put her hands on either side of his gorgeous face. Standing on her tippy-toes she tilted her neck to nip at his lips with her teeth. She tasted the salty breeze on them with her tongue.

"Candy," he groaned, wrapping his large hands on her ass, pulling her against his erection, grinding her against him.

She sank to the sandy floor and he descended with her, their lips and tongues still entwined in a sensuous dance.

"You didn't actually think I was going to let that huge cock of yours go to waste, did you?" she asked him, mirth twinkling in her large brown eyes as she unzipped his pants and pulled out his throbbing penis.

Rolling him over onto his back, she crawled up on top of him, stroking the velvet skin on his hard-as-steel cock as she did so. He reached up under her skirt and roughly pulled the motorized thong from her hips. She moved her legs to help him get the panties off.

She licked her lips and with great concentration kneeled above his cock and guided it into her wet hole with her hand. He leaned up to kiss her and as their lips found each other, she began to ride him with a ferocity that was more than he could handle after already watching her explode twice in her seat at the restaurant.

Her tight, slick cunt sucked his cock so thoroughly he knew he was going to blow. Wanting to take her with him he slid his hand up under her skirt and pressed his thumb against her engorged clit.

Together, they fell into a gulf of intense pleasure, kissing each other frantically, thrashing heedlessly against each other as they climbed higher and higher on the soft sand floor of their private love shack.

Chapter Nine

After shaking his hand and saying, "Thank you for a wonderful lesson," Candace got into her car and drove away.

Charlie stood in the parking lot and watched her leave. He was unaccountably disappointed. He had hoped that maybe they had progressed beyond the handshake. Hell, he'd thought they had progressed beyond a handshake the minute she started stripping off her clothes and he had pressed his tongue to her eager clit.

He ran his hands through his hair and walked out onto the beach, sitting down on an old log. He knew what was happening to him and it scared the shit out of him.

Good old Charlie Gibson, writer extraordinaire of erotic romance, who hadn't had a serious girlfriend since his messy divorce five years earlier, was falling in love.

And he didn't have a clue how to tell the object of his affection how he felt.

"So much for being good with dialogue," he muttered into the wind and let the waves carry his words away.

* * * * *

Candace drove home from the restaurant Monday night still wearing the remote controlled thong, with the controls stashed neatly in her little purse along with her silk panties. A balloon of joy was swelling up inside of her chest.

Being with Charlie made her feel good. Okay, so being with him made her pussy feel incredibly good, but it was more than just the sexual rush she got whenever he was near her.

When she was with Charlie, she felt like the best of her was actually breaking out. The walls she had built up around her heart to protect herself from pain were falling, one by one, and even though she was frightened about what lay ahead, she wasn't sorry that she had embarked on this crazy ride with Charlie.

My mentor, she thought, and laughed wickedly, thinking about how upset Sheba, Queen of the Sluts, would be if she knew just how hot and hands-on Charlie's version of mentoring actually was.

But in addition to all of the personal revelations Candace was having, she also felt more inspired to write than she ever had before. And as soon as she parked her car and let herself inside the door, she headed straight to her office and booted up her computer.

Pausing for just a moment to gather her

thoughts, she began to type furiously, the words coming out as fast as a hard rain.

Jolene felt her innocence falling off of her in thick sheets. Every time she exploded in Zane's arms, she changed just a little bit more. But still, twenty-one years of Catholic School training was hard to get rid of, no matter how powerful her orgasms were, no matter how much she loved the feel of his thick cock between her legs.

All day, she had been working with the local Catholic church, helping the choir get ready for their annual performance, and she couldn't help but wonder if she had fallen in with the devil.

It wasn't the first time this thought had occurred to her. Surrounded by all of the pure, untouched young girls and the solemn nun who was conducting the practice, Jolene felt dirty. As if she didn't deserve to feel the way she felt when Zane was in the room with her.

No, it was worse than that. All she had to do was think about Zane, think about his full lips, the way his stubble scratched her breasts, the tender skin on the inside of her thighs, and her panties instantly got wet.

That kind of thing only happened to bad girls. And although Jolene had made a conscious decision to stray from the path of perfection, she wondered if she had strayed too far.

Now, as she stood in front of the door to "Piano Man", she was tempted to turn and run as fast as she could back to the life she used to live.

The door flew open, and Zane's large, muscular body filled the frame. "Why are you skulking around outside?" he asked irately. "You know I don't like you hanging around by yourself in this neighborhood."

Jolene scowled at him. It felt so good to give in to her natural emotions instead of always caging her responses in politeness.

"Ha! That's a good one," she replied in a snotty voice. "I'd like to know how anyone on the street is going to do anything worse to me than the things you've already made me do!"

His eyes narrowed at her sarcastic comment and roughly he grabbed her by the arm and hauled her inside. Pushing her up against the wall, he shoved one of his leather-clad thighs between her legs and pinned her arms up against the wall.

"Are you actually telling me that you think I made you grab my head so that you could rub your cunt all over my tongue?"

She whimpered as his hands tightened on her wrists. She was aware of the huge bulge in Zane's tight leather pants pressing up against her hip, and she couldn't believe how much she wanted him to unzip his pants and plunge into her until she couldn't see or breathe or even speak.

"Do you expect me to believe that I made you so sensitive that the slightest touch of my tongue on your clit makes you scream? That I'm to blame because you are so hot and ready all the time

all I have to do is slide into your pussy an inch and you lose control?"

The way he growled the questions at her, Jolene was almost afraid to respond. Frankly, she wasn't sure what the right answer was anymore.

But before she could say anything, he cursed and shoved away from her. "I bought a present for you."

Jolene's face lit up and she started to move towards him, saying, "You did? Can I see what it is?" but the look he gave her was so fierce she instinctively backed up against the wall again, as if she could hide in between the studs that held the building up.

Rationally, she knew he would never hurt her—he was too gentle, too intent on giving her pleasure—but by the look in his eyes at the moment, she wasn't sure she knew him at all.

He walked behind the bar and pulled out a plastic bag. "If I give this to you, do you promise to do exactly what I tell you to do?"

Jolene laughed and sassed back at him, "When have I not done exactly what you've told me to do, boss?" She felt like she was back on solid ground as she waited for him to give her the present.

He tossed the bag over the counter at her and she caught it right before it knocked over one of the tea-lights on a table. "Can I open it right now?"

He shook his head. "Go to the bathroom,

*and when you come back out to play, I want you to
be wearing what's in the bag."*

*She cocked her head at him in confusion.
"You bought me clothes? What's wrong with what I
have on?" she asked as she gestured to her sky blue
cocktail dress.*

*"Nothing," he replied, "as long as you have
a thing for nuns." He shook his head. "Just go. The
bar's about to open."*

*As he turned back to getting the bar ready
for the busy evening ahead, Jolene headed for the
bathroom. Barely staving off her curiosity, she
walked into the ladies room and locked the door
behind her. Opening up the bag all she saw was an
itty-bitty scrap of black fabric and wondered just
what kind of game Zane was playing with her.*

*"He can't actually expect me to put this
on!" she exclaimed as she picked up what looked to
be a pair of underwear. She had heard about thongs
but had never worn a pair of them herself. They
seemed much too slutty and besides, they didn't
seem the least bit comfortable.*

*She wondered what Zane would do if she
didn't put the thong on. "He'll never know," she
whispered, but at the same time, she knew he never
did anything without a reason, and the rapidly
emerging bad-girl in her wondered what his reason
was.*

*At the least, she knew he would make her
feel incredibly good when the last customer had left
for the night and it was just the two of them. She*

still blushed at the thought of how she had let him penetrate her with the mouth of a beer bottle the previous night. Not that it didn't make her scream with joy, of course, it was just that the whole thing seemed a little crazy.

Jolene was pretty sure that being with a good girl like her was a new experience for Zane, even though she was getting to be more and more of an ex-good-girl with every night she spent at the "Piano Man". By the looks of the women who threw themselves at him night after night—trashy hair, too-tight jeans, caked-on makeup—she figured the only reason he was with her was because she was a novelty.

If his reaction to finding out she was a virgin that first night was anything to go by, he was definitely in uncharted territory. After his release, she could have sworn he was about to apologize to her for taking advantage of her, but she couldn't stand to hear him say he was sorry about the best thing that had ever happened to her, so she kissed him before he could say the words.

She refocused on the thong she was holding between her thumb and index finger. "What the heck," she said. "If he wants me to wear a thong, I'll wear a thong. And he'll be the only person who knows."

It was a little exciting, she thought, for him to know she was hardly wearing any underwear underneath her ankle-length dress.

She slipped off her white cotton panties and

*pulled the small slip of material up around her hips.
It felt as if there was something firm tucked up
around her vagina lips, and she shrugged, figuring
all thongs came with plastic in the crotch, for extra
support, perhaps?*

*She walked back into the bar and handed
Zane the plastic bag. He opened it, and when he
saw her white cotton underpants lying in the bottom
of the bag, he smiled. Jolene headed for the piano
to warm up, and when she sat down on the piano
stool she was distinctly aware of a pressure against
her clitoris.*

*She stole a glance at Zane, and wondered if
this is what he had planned for her, but he was on
the phone and didn't so much as look at her.*

*Jolene smiled a small smile and felt the tips
of her breasts tingling behind her white cotton bra.
Now that she knew Zane wanted her to play piano
all night for his customers with a solid reminder of
what was to come later pressing against her
already swollen flesh, it took a great deal of effort
for her to concentrate on playing scales to warm up
her fingers.*

*An hour later she was playing the chorus to
Billy Joel's "Piano Man", which had just been
requested by one of the regulars, when she felt
something funny happening between her legs. She
missed a note and then quickly covered with a vamp
up the ivory keyboard to make it sound like she was
playing Billy's song wrong on purpose.*

Then she felt it again, a quick jolt of energy

pulsing against her clit. She looked up in confusion, but she didn't lose her place in the song this time. Zane was standing behind the bar watching her carefully.

What the heck is wrong with these panties, she wondered as she played into the last rousing chorus of the song. Suddenly, the buzzing started up again between her thighs, but this time she knew that somehow, some way, Zane was manning the controls to her cunt.

As her nipples grew rock-hard and incredibly sensitive, as her clitoris grew engorged by the stimulation of the vibrating thong, she played louder and louder, faster and faster, hoping the booming piano would mask the whimpers that escaped her as wave upon wave of pleasure shook her to her very core.

When the orgasm had finished ripping through her and she played the final line of the song, she paused for a moment to catch her breath, staring unseeingly at the song sheets in front of her.

She now knew two things for sure.

Zane Michels was, indeed, the devil.

And she, Jolene Mackenzie, had most definitely strayed onto the path of evil.

Candace saved her document and looked up through the window of her office just as the sun was rising in the night sky. She slumped back against her chair feeling equal parts pride and remorse.

On the one hand, she was writing the best

damn erotica of her life. On the other hand, with every page she wrote, she felt guiltier and guiltier about abusing Charlie's trust. The problem was simple: She may have promised not to reveal the content of their lessons to anyone, but once the words started to come to her, she couldn't stop herself.

It was just how she felt when she was with Charlie.

Completely, utterly out of control.

* * * * *

Done with her writing for the day, Candace picked up the pile of bills and magazines and took them into the kitchen with her. The words EROTICA CONTEST caught her eye and she pulled the leaflet out from the stack of envelopes and read:

Do you have an erotic manuscript that would knock our panties off? If so, you should enter the 15th annual Erotic Writer's Contest. If your manuscript makes it to the finals, your book will be read by a panel of top editors. A secret celebrity judge will present the winner his or her award, along with a $10,000 grand prize check! Enter now!

Candace usually threw contest solicitations out, but that was because she knew she didn't have something that could win. The wheels started turning in her head.

"No," she said aloud in her empty kitchen. "I can't do it. It's not right."

The wicked little voice inside her said, *Come on Candace. You know you've got a winner on your hands. Charlie will never know.*

She tried to ignore the voice, but it just got louder, saying, *This is the entire reason he agreed to be your mentor. Charlie wants you to become a better writer. After all, isn't that the only reason why he's sleeping with you?*

Candace wanted to argue, she wanted to tell her nasty inner-voice that Charlie was sleeping with her because he cared about her, but in her experience, that was never what was really going on.

Using her past hurts as her guide, tapping into her failed love affairs to try and cover up the strong feelings she had for Charlie, she picked up her phone and dialed his number.

She needed to schedule lesson four, and fast. After all, she had a book to finish and there was only one way she could get the experience she needed.

In Charlie Gibson's arms.

Chapter Ten

Charlie was pleased that Candace had called him to arrange lesson four so quickly. *Maybe she likes me a little bit after all,* he thought to himself.

The only problem was, he hadn't quite figured out an appropriate site for their lesson on sex in new locations. Dodging her questions on the phone, he told her he'd pick her up at noon on Thursday and surprise her with their destination.

He ran through the options again in his head. A sex club was too predictable, and there was no way in hell he'd let anyone else get his hands on her. Doing it in his car, parked out over a beautiful vista, was too much like being in high school. Having a quickie in a dark alley on a busy street was straight out of his latest novel, so that was out of the question.

With only fifteen minutes to go until he was supposed to be at Candace's house, he still hadn't come up with a good location for their lesson.

"Where is the one place she'd never think about having sex?" he asked himself in frustrated tones.

The answer came to him in a flash.

Charlie smiled, grabbed his keys, and hopped in his red Z3 BMW convertible, turning up Aerosmith so loud he could feel the bass drum vibrating in his seat.

* * * * *

"The zoo?"

Candace turned to him with a look of utter surprise.

Charlie paid for their tickets and followed her into the park. "Yup," he said, nodding happily. "The zoo."

She shook her head and chuckled. "You have got to be kidding. I'd like to know one thing that's sexy about the zoo."

He pulled her close and said, "You," before kissing her hard on her lips. Grabbing her hand, he said, "Let's go ride the train around the park."

She raised an eyebrow, but followed after him. "You're the teacher, so I guess you know best," she said, but he could tell by the sound of her voice that she thought he was completely nuts.

The zoo grounds were deserted at noon on a Thursday and as they walked hand-in-hand, Charlie thought again how much he loved being with Candace. She was funny, witty, smart, and incredibly passionate. For a moment, he almost wished they were done with their lessons so that he could finally tell her how he felt about her, without feeling like a total jerk for taking advantage of their teacher/student situation.

But then he thought about what he had planned for the day and grinned. No, he certainly didn't want to give up any of the time he'd be spending exploring Candace's body. And he sure as hell wouldn't trade the satisfaction he'd already received from showing her how to let herself go, how to explode with every fiber of her body and soul.

They walked past the tiger and lion cages, stopping to admire the brawny beasts, finally arriving at the miniature train depot. One of the small amusement park trains was on the track waiting for them to board.

Each of the cars of the train was just big enough to seat two people, except the miniature lion cage, which was barely big enough to fit four people.

"Wait here for a second," Charlie said as he went up to the ticket taker and said a few words to him while covertly slipping him a hundred dollar bill.

Mission accomplished, Charlie was grinning ear to ear when he waved Candace through the gate.

She started to step into one of the small, uncovered cars that was shaped like a baby elephant, but he redirected her to the lion cage. The bottom half of the car was completely covered with plastic, with only the upper half of the car open to the outside through thick plastic bars. Unlike the other cars, this one had a roof on it that blocked out the sunlight.

"We're going to ride in this one," he said, and he thought he saw a tiny hint of a smile appearing on the corner of her luscious lips as she crawled into the small space.

When she bent over, her short skirt flipped up and revealed her tight, round ass, and smooth pussy lips peeking between her slightly parted thighs.

His cock went instantly hard. His innocent student hadn't worn any panties at all!

He stood on the outside of the cage, holding onto the bars and cleared his throat, finally managing a husky, "Did you forget to put something on this morning when you were getting dressed?"

Candace blushed and said, "I might have forgotten a couple of things, actually."

Suddenly he noticed she wasn't wearing a bra either. He could discern the faint outline of her areolas beneath her light pink tank top. As he stared at her chest in continued amazement, her nipples grew hard and pronounced, and it was all he could do not to rip the thin fabric off of her body and suck at her nipples like a hungry newborn.

He rearranged his pants to accommodate his throbbing bulge and climbed in after her. Once he was inside the cage and had latched the gate closed, he gave a thumb's up to the conductor and the train began to move slowly on the tracks.

"You seem a little nervous today," he said as

he rubbed his thumb in a circle over the palm of her left hand.

She nodded, but didn't quite meet his eyes. Finally, she looked up at him and said, "You're right. I am nervous today." Then she laughed and said, "Which is crazy. You'd think I'd be perfectly calm around you after the three lessons we've had so far, wouldn't you?"

Charlie nodded absentmindedly as he kneeled in the small floor space between her legs. "I'm a little nervous too," he murmured as he slowly slid his hands up from her ankles, to her knees, to the outsides of her thighs.

"Lift up," he said softly and as she did so, he slid his hands underneath the curve of her ass, cupping each of her butt cheeks in his hands. Her head fell back and she moaned softly. He'd left her skirt still covering her body, even though he wanted nothing more than to bury his face between her legs, hoping the waiting would intensify her arousal.

Even though his hands were on her ass, she was already so wet her juices were soaking his fingers. Gently he slipped his pinkies into her dripping cunt and her moans grew louder. Her hands moved to circle the back of his neck, to pull his face down to her impatient clit.

"Hold onto the bars," he demanded. He saw her warring with herself, but then she reached out and grabbed the bars with her hands.

"Good girl," he whispered as he bit the hem of her tank top and pulled it up several inches to uncover the skin on her flat stomach. He laid several kisses across her belly, and then on her pelvis through the thin fabric of her skirt.

Her nipples jutted out to him and he couldn't resist their beckoning. One at a time, he put the thin straps of her tank top between his teeth and slid them down her shoulders, uncovering first one lush globe and then the other. He moved his hands closer to her pussy and slid several fingers in and out of her.

"Charlie, I don't think we should-" she began to say, and he cut off her protest with a hot kiss, roughly taking her tongue into his mouth, forcing it to mate with his own.

"I'm in charge of this lesson," he said sternly when he finally pulled away from her slightly bruised lips.

She said, "I know you are, but-" and he kissed her again, gently this time just on the corners of her mouth

"Won't you trust me, sweetheart?" he asked her, his tone now gently cajoling.

She smiled tremulously and he returned his attention to her succulent tits, finally bared in all their glory. He rubbed his face across them, letting her nipples slide in and out of his mouth, driving his tongue across them, forcing whimpers from Candace with every stroke.

Looking up from her breasts, he noted that the train had taken them into a deeply forested area, which was far more private than the open tracks they had traveled upon thus far. As he slowly pulled his hands out from beneath her ass and reached for the hem of her skirt to lift it up, she whimpered, "Yes, Charlie. Please!" and opened her legs wide so that he would have easy access to her swollen cunt. He ran the tip of his thumb up and down her moist folds, steering clear of her most sensitive spot. She tried to maneuver her hips so that he'd be forced to touch her clit, but he teased and circled, all the while avoiding the one place that was dying for his touch.

He slid one finger into her and sucked her nipple in the same rhythm as he moved his long finger in and out of her.

Candace's head thrashed back and forth and she let go of the bars to wrap her hands around the back of his head, holding him tightly to her breasts. He could feel the tension in her body, felt the muscles begin to convulse around his finger, and knew she was about to explode.

Hastily he removed his finger and, with his lips still sucking gently on one of her breasts, Charlie moved to a sitting position on the hard plastic seat behind him, bringing Candace's body with him, so that she was straddling his hips, her knees on the seat.

Her slender fingers moved to unbutton and unzip his khaki slacks, until the full length of his hard shaft sprang free.

She wrapped her hand around the hot length of him, positioning herself above him so that the head of his penis was just at the entrance of her incredibly wet lips.

With a sound of deep satisfaction, Candace lowered herself down onto his cock, taking in each and every inch.

Charlie was overwhelmed by the sensation of her tight, wet pussy enveloping him. He looked up from her breasts, and pulled her head down to capture her mouth in a hot, tongue-thrusting kiss.

Candace was in charge of their lovemaking as she rode up and down on Charlie's cock, milking it with her tight, throbbing muscles.

"I can't hold on anymore," he gritted out through clenched teeth and as he began to come, her muscles convulsed around his cock. He covered her cry of pleasure with his mouth and as they rode towards ecstasy together, their lips and tongues mated in a frenzy that matched the mating of their bodies.

As their convulsions came to an end, they kissed, their caresses growing tender and soft.

"Candy, I-" Charlie began to say, but right as he was about to declare his feelings for her, regardless of their mentor/mentee relationship, the train left the trees and emerged back into the daylight.

Quickly, Candace slid off his lap, pulled her tank top back up over her breasts, and slid her skirt down over her thighs. After she did so she looked at him with undisguised amusement. "You might want to zip your pants back up."

He surfaced from his daze and made his fumbling fingers obey his commands to tuck in his shirt. Just in time, he fastened the button of his pants as they arrived back at the station and came to a stop.

The station attendant unlatched the door to their cage. "Enjoy the ride?"

Candace looked at Charlie with a twinkle in her eye and said, with a fairly straight face, "Oh yes. More than you can ever imagine. In fact, it's safe to say, I'll never look at the zoo the same way again."

And with that, she headed out the gates back towards the lion cages. Both Charlie and the young zoo employee watched the perfect curve of her ass swing from side to side as she walked.

Charlie slipped the kid another $100 bill and said, "You really have a great ride on your hands here, kid. You got a girlfriend?"

The boy nodded his head speedily on his skinny neck and Charlie said, "I definitely recommend the lion cage." He followed after Candace, thinking yet again what a lucky man he was.

Chapter Eleven

When Charlie dropped Candace off at her house, she was torn between inviting him in and running to her computer to write down the next scene in her book. But before she could ask him inside for a drink, he looked at his watch and said, "I've got to get going. Thanks for a great afternoon," and sped off, leaving her standing on the sidewalk in front of her house feeling more than a little bereft.

The truth was, no matter how much she tried to pretend she didn't have feelings for Charlie, no matter how much she wavered back and forth about the emotional extent of their relationship, she now knew with 100% certainty that she was in love with him.

After their incredible sex play on the mini-train at the zoo, they had spent the rest of the day eating cotton candy and hot dogs, riding the elephants, and admiring the baby tiger cubs that were brought outside during their feeding. With every minute that passed in Charlie's company, Candace fell harder and harder for him.

He was funny, gorgeous, brilliant, and the most sexually intoxicating man she had ever encountered. Candace was sure she would never meet anyone again who would make her feel so incredibly good, so wonderfully happy.

All of that only served to increase her guilt over her deception. Every time she wrote another scene with Jolene and Zane, she was elated by how far she'd come as a writer. But at the same time, another part of her was horrified by her dishonesty.

To a moan, every scene mimicked her encounters with Charlie.

She went inside her house, sat down in front of her computer and booted it up, holding her head in her hands, trying to figure out some sort of compromise she could live with.

What if I tell him about the story after we've cemented a strong relationship with each other outside of his mentoring?

If he wanted to have a real relationship with her, then by the time she told him about the story she had written, he'd just laugh and kiss her, telling her she was silly for even worrying about it in the first place.

She wasn't going to keep it a secret from him forever. Just until she entered the contest and got some feedback on her writing. Just until she and Charlie communicated with each other about their feelings.

Feeling slightly better about what she was doing, she opened up her document and typed the

words she had been writing in her head all
afternoon.

"You ever been on a motorcycle?"
Jolene looked up from the piano keys at
Zane who was standing by the front door of the bar.
"Are you kidding? I've never even been in a
convertible," she replied.
"We're gonna open a little late today," he
said, gesturing for her to come to him. "Let's go."
Zane held the door open for Jolene and
tapped his booted foot impatiently while she
serenely closed the lid on the grand piano, stood up
and walked towards him.
He led her around the back to his Harley
and handed her a helmet. She swallowed nervously
and didn't put the helmet on.
"I'm not so sure about this," she said, but
he was already on and had revved up the engine.
"You'll be just fine," he said, "just keep
your arms wrapped tightly around me."
Jolene felt like she had no choice but to do
as he asked. It was always that way with Zane, she
mused. Him telling and her doing.
"One day the tables are going to turn,
Zane," she said, but he couldn't hear her over the
rumbling of his engine.
She slipped onto the seat behind him and
wiggled her hips tightly up against his muscled rear
end and thighs. She ran her hands up and down his
chiseled abs through his t-shirt and reveled in his

extraordinary masculinity.

And then they were off, flying down the streets of San Francisco. The wind whipped at her hair and with her body wrapped around Zane's, she felt perfectly in tune with the world around her. Every person who walked by them seemed to be smiling. The sky was bluer. The sun was hotter.

Of course, her pussy was completely soaked. It was such a frequent occurrence, she had stopped wearing panties altogether. As it was, whenever she was with Zane he was always ripping them off of her in his haste to thrust his huge shaft into her or to press his lips to the sensitive nub between her legs.

She had only worked for him for a month, but already she knew she wouldn't have it any other way. Zane was a drug she never wanted to get off of, no matter how wrong anyone thought he might be for her.

She had gone home once to visit her parents, and she couldn't believe how hard it was for her to pull her hair back into a ponytail and sit quietly at dinner. All night while she was with her parents she wondered what Zane was doing, wondered what he would have done to her at the end of the evening after he locked the door to his bar.

After catching her in a daydream more than once, her mother pulled her aside in the kitchen to ask if anything was the matter. Jolene knew she had to get back to the city right away, back to the man whose caresses had become as important to her as breathing.

Eventually, the road dead-ended into Golden Gate Park. Zane slowed down the bike and drove into a thickly forested, deserted area. Jolene shivered with anticipation, hoping Zane was going to start touching, licking, and biting her soon.

I am a slut, she thought. Wholly and completely a slut. But by now, after so many nights of falling to pieces in Zane's arms, she was too far gone to care about something that would have bothered her deeply in her past life.

He pulled off his helmet and his shoulder-length dark brown hair whipped gently against her face in the wind. She took off her helmet and shook out her long blond hair, trying to finger-comb the knots out to no avail. Still balanced on the bike seat she leaned her head back and closed her eyes, letting the gentle breeze wash over her.

Zane stood up and got off of his bike, turning around to face her as he straddled the seat once again.

"Oh!" she exclaimed nervously when she opened up her eyes. His face was directly in front of hers, his eyes hot with need.

He bent his head down and captured her lips in a sweet kiss. Reaching under her skirt, he ran his hands slowly up her calves, past her knees, up to her thighs.

When he finally reached her hips, he stopped kissing her and gave her a searing look.

"You're not wearing panties," he said.

She gave him a half-smile, saying, "I was wondering when you'd notice."

He growled and kissed her again, hungrily, slipping his large callused hands beneath her ass, lifting her up off the seat and onto him. She felt the thick bulge in his pants and reached for the button of his jeans.

He chuckled softly. "We're in public, you know," he said.

Unable, unwilling to stop herself, Jolene worked at his fly. "Isn't that the point, Zane?"

By then she had his pants undone and as his shaft sprang free into her hands, she was pleased to find that he wasn't wearing anything underneath his jeans.

As she stroked the satiny skin of his huge cock, he groaned, saying, "What did you do with my little nun?"

Jolene wriggled onto Zane's lap and gasped as his hot flesh probed her pussy lips, stretching her open to fit all of him inside. After he was sheathed to the hilt within her, she looked him in the eye.

"I love you, Zane," she said, and then instinctively rode up and down on his cock, faster and faster as her orgasm swelled up to overwhelm her.

Zane kept the bike steady while she took him in and then slid him out until just the tip was still within her. He pulled her down on him again, so deeply she could feel his balls press against her ass cheeks. At the feel of him swelling impossibly bigger within her, she went over the edge, crying out his name as her inner muscles clenched and milked him hard.

He buried his head in her long hair and roared, "Jolene!" as he shot inside of her, crashing his hips into hers as hard and deep as he could.

They held tight to each other until their heartbeats returned to normal, and then he slid her off of him and zipped up his jeans. Without a word, he handed Jolene her helmet, put his back on, and started the engine.

Jolene blinked back tears. When they were joined together she realized she could no longer deny how much she loved Zane and was unable to hold back the words.

But now they were heading back to the bar and he hadn't said anything. Not, "I love you too," or any kind of comment at all in response to her open and honest statement of her feelings for him. With a sinking feeling low in her belly, she wondered if she had done the wrong thing.

Maybe, she thought with sudden sorrow, loving the devil is nothing more than a one-way trip to hell.

Candace finished writing her new scene and as she reread it, she had a spark of insight about the piece of the puzzle between her and Charlie that she had been missing all along.

It was one thing for her to learn to enjoy

taking pleasure in Charlie's arms—lots and lots of pleasure!—but it was another thing entirely for her to lead the way.

Her path was suddenly crystal clear and she wanted to jump for joy. Lesson five was going to be different than the previous four lessons, for one big reason.

She was going to be the teacher this time.

Decision made, she grabbed her car keys, and locked the front door behind her. If everything went according to plan, she wouldn't be coming home tonight.

* * * * *

Charlie sat in his living room and stared blankly at the TV. "I'm such an idiot," he told himself, taking a large swig from the beer he'd pulled out the six-pack by his side.

"She was going to ask me to come inside, probably to her bedroom, and I act like a sixteen-year-old boy!"

He shook his head at his stupidity. He couldn't believe how nervous he got around Candace whenever it came time to wrap up their lessons. That he was still afraid she'd say, "Thanks so much for everything, and by the way, I never want to see you again, you pervert."

He wanted so desperately to tell her he was in love with her, even though he had only known her less than two weeks. As it was, the fact that they had mind-blowing sex during each of the lessons was a little weird, but at least they had an upfront agreement about it: Whatever happened during their lessons, stayed in their lessons.

If only they had made some sort of agreement about their emotions. Something like: *If I fall in love with you, I can tell you how I feel and you'll say you've fallen in love with me too.*

Charlie sighed and flipped the top off another bottle. Getting drunk was the sucker's way out, but since that's what he was, he drank up.

A knock on his door startled him out of his not-quite-drunken-enough stupor. He plopped the beer bottle down, sloshing sticky liquid all over the coffee table, and dragged himself to the door.

"Probably some kid trying to sell candy bars," he muttered as he turned the doorknob.

"Hey Charlie!" Candace said, as she stood on his doorstep looking more glorious than any angel ever had. "Could I come in?"

He nodded and stepped aside dazedly.

She was still wearing the short yellow skirt and pink top from their jaunt to the zoo. She looked tastier than ever, especially since the zippy night air had puckered her nipples up beneath her thin cotton tank.

She turned to him with a determined look in her eyes. "I was thinking about lesson five, and all of the wonderful lessons we've already had. I think we need to shake things up a little bit for this last lesson. So, for lesson five, which I believe you told me was going to be about role playing, I'm going to be the teacher and you're going to be the student."

Charlie's cock stood up at attention as he took in her words. He was speechless, stunned that she had magically appeared on his doorstep, mesmerized by her beauty, and bowled over by how she wanted to reverse their roles.

Not waiting for any response for him, she walked out of his foyer and down the hall, until she reached the door of his master bedroom. She looked over her shoulder and said, "You don't want to be late to class, do you? 'Cause I hear the teacher spanks her students when they're bad," and then disappeared into his bedroom.

By the time he snapped out of his fog and jogged down the hall to the goddess who awaited him, Candace was nowhere to be found in his bedroom. Hearing the water running in his adjoining bathroom, he peeked his head into the doorway and saw a blessed sight.

Candace was leaning over his enormous spa bathtub, setting the water temperature and jets.

And she was completely, blessedly naked.

He reached for the hem of his t-shirt to pull it off over his head, but she whipped around and said, "Keep your clothes on."

He stopped with the shirt mid-way up his torso. "Huh?"

She walked up to him and pressed her full breasts up against his chest. "You heard me. I want you to keep your clothes on until I tell you otherwise," she said, and then spun around and gingerly dipped a toe into the hot water. Slipping into the tub, she stretched out fully, with her nipples jutting proudly out of the water. They puckered tightly as cool air blew across them.

"Soap me up," she said, and Charlie immediately gathered up a small washcloth and a bar of herbal soap off the holder by the sink.

"Kneel on the bath mat," she directed him, and again he did as she bade. Then she crossed her legs in the tub and wiggled the toes on her right foot. "Start here."

Incredibly aroused by the way she had taken charge of their lovemaking, Charlie thought his cock was going to explode in his pants. He wet the small, soft terry cloth towel, slid it over the bar of soap until it foamed, and rubbed it over the arch of her foot, making her moan with pleasure.

He worked the cloth diligently up her right leg, leaning over the rim of the sunken two-person tub to touch every inch of her smooth skin, running the cloth past her kneecap, across the top of her thigh. And then, just as he got to the apex between her legs, he stopped, lathered up the towel and started with her left foot, mirroring his actions on her left side.

"Wash me, student."

Charlie held back a grin and obeyed her again, pressing the cloth firmly into her pussy lips, rubbing it back and forth over her clit, watching her nipples grow engorged as she got more and more aroused, watching the pulse in her neck beat wildly as she closed her eyes and arched her back.

She came undone beneath his hand.

He wanted to kiss her, but he knew she was in charge of this lesson, so he continued to rock her pelvis in the palm of his hand until her breathing returned to normal and she opened her eyes again.

"Take off your clothes and get inside the tub," she said evenly.

He was surprised by how controlled she was, considering she had been screaming and writhing just moments before.

He quickly stripped off his t-shirt and jeans and then stepped into the warm water. He stood in the tub, his cock thick and hard and ready to plunge into Candace's dripping cunt.

"Don't you dare come until I tell you to," she said as she kneeled in the tub and while he was still standing up, she took the head of his cock into her mouth lightly ran her tongue over it, tasting him.

Then she slid more of his penis into her mouth and he felt his head pushing up against the back of her throat. She sucked against his shaft while she held his balls in her hands.

"Candy, I won't be able to-" he began to say when he didn't think he could take it any longer, and she took her sweet lips off of his cock and pulled him down into the tub.

"Do me doggy," she said, and turned over so that her breasts were pressed up against the cool tile surrounding the tub and her ass was flared up from the rim.

Charlie kneeled behind her. "If the teacher insists."

He reached one hand around between the tile and her torso to cup and squeeze her breasts and the other around to swirl her swollen clit.

And then he did what he'd wanted to do since the beginning of lesson one, and rammed his cock hard into Candace's pussy.

His balls were swinging into her thighs and she reached around to cup them in her hands. "Harder, Charlie. Harder!" she demanded as she pushed her ass tighter to his hips, wiggling and moaning.

He couldn't remember the last time his cock had been so distended, so engorged. As he felt his cock begin to contract, he pressed his palm against her swollen, firm clit and pumped his hand against her mound.

"Oh god, Candy, you're so hot, so wet," he groaned.

The water was cold by the time she wrung the last drop of come out of him. They untangled their bodies and got up to take a shower.

As he dried her off with a thick towel, she smiled at him and said, "Thanks for the five great mentoring sessions," and kissed him softly on his lips, letting her tongue merge with his.

Pulling back from her mouth, Charlie said, "Candy, there's something I need to tell you," at the very exact time she said, "Charlie, there's something I've been meaning to say to you."

They laughed and kissed again. "You first," he said, and tried to get his heart to stop pounding so damn hard in his chest as he waited for her to speak.

Suddenly looking shy and unsure, she forced herself to look into his eyes and said, "First of all, I want you to know how much I've enjoyed working with you this week. And even though I know these were just supposed to be lessons for me to write better erotica, the truth is..."

Her words fell away and Charlie swallowed hard once.

Taking a deep breath she started again. "The truth is, Charlie, I'm in love with you."

Charlie had never been happier. He put his arms around her waist and spun her around in a circle in his large bathroom, their towels falling into a heap on the floor.

Breathless with joy, he said, "Candy, I love you too, and it's been killing me not telling you all week."

She reached her hands up around the back of his head and kissed him passionately. He swept her up into his arms, walked into the bedroom, and laid her on his bed.

Where she belonged.

* * * * *

"Nothing is ever going to come between us," Charlie said thickly and Candace covered his mouth with hers before he could see the guilt and worry in her eyes.

I'll tell him about the story soon, she promised herself as she sank deeper into the comfort of Charlie's arms.

Chapter Twelve

Candace thought back on the incredible night she and Charlie had spent together and smiled, happier than she had ever been. She had taken charge of her own sexuality for once in her life, and told the man she loved how she felt. And to add to the perfection, he felt the same way!

He had wanted her to spend the weekend with him, and she was tempted, but she wanted to finish her story first so that she could overnight it to the judges. Making an excuse about some errands, she promised to be back in his bed by the evening.

Sitting down at her desk, Candace knew exactly how her story needed to end.

Zane watched Jolene play the piano and reminded himself again that his relationship with her would never last, that they came from different worlds, that he would eventually tire of her body.

He was full of shit. Any fool could tell that he was completely, irrevocably, ridiculously in love with the angel-faced girl who sat so primly at the piano in his bar and played jazz standards with all her heart.

The girl who looked like a nun, but made love like a she-devil.

As he served a trio of overly made up, cheaply dressed women sitting at the bar trying to get his attention, he winced and thought about how they used to be just the kind of women he would take home and fuck. Now, just the thought of being with any woman but Jolene disgusted him.

By the time the bar closed that night, he had never been more ready to lock the doors and take Jolene into his arms. But when he looked around the bar for her, she was nowhere to be found.

"Damn it!" he said, angry at her for leaving him alone when he needed her most.

Walking into his office, he found a note on his desk. "Zane. I've never stolen anything in my life, but I took the keys to your house and I'll be waiting there for you, if you want to join me. Jolene."

He stroked the prickly stubble on his chin and wondered what she was up to. They had been in his house only once, on the way home from the bar, before he dropped her off at her apartment. She knows damn well we only fuck here, in the bar, *he thought angrily.*

He didn't want to take her to his bed where he had screwed so many other, meaningless women.

Jolene was special.

He drove his Harley home as if he were a Hell's Angel. He stomped loudly up his front stairs, hoping he was scaring her just a bit. She was going

*to get the spanking of her life from him once he got
inside, and his cock hardened as he thought of her
soft flesh beneath the palm of his hand. He could
already see her ass turning pink under his assault,
and could taste her come on his lips.*

*He turned the knob and the door opened.
"Jolene," he called, but got no answer. She wasn't
in his living room or the kitchen, so he walked down
the hall and heard the water running in his master
bath.*

*When he walked into the room, his little nun
was lying naked beneath the hot water, smiling
wickedly.*

*He was so angry and so aroused he
growled, "What the hell are you doing?" but she
just sank deeper into the water and said, "I want
you to soap me up."*

"You what?" he exploded.

*She shook her head at him and pinched her
lips into a tight line of disapproval. "You heard me.
Soap me up.*

*"The hell I'm going to," he said, and she
rose up angrily out of the tub.*

*"You big jerk," she cried as water poured
off her naked body. "I'm asking you to do one
simple thing, and all you do is use blasphemy!" She
made a fist and said, "Now get over here and do as
I say!"*

*Zane leaned against the door, crossed his
arms, and said, "Make me."*

Narrowing her eyes at him, Jolene stepped

*out of the tub. Walking towards him, she grabbed a
towel off of the rack and threw it onto the floor in
front of his black boots. Kneeling in front of him she
undid the button on his jeans and unzipped the
zipper, letting his cock spring free of its overly tight
confines.*

*Jolene had never taken him into her mouth
before. Because she was such a novice, he'd never
forced her to blow him, happy to sink into her tight,
wet pussy every night instead.*

*He was shocked by her new brazen
behavior. His arousal was so acute he was afraid
he'd shoot into her mouth the minute she so much
as kissed the head of his cock.*

*Running her fingers up and down his penis,
she stuck the tip of her sweet little tongue out and
licked him once, twice, and then suddenly sucked in
several inches of him, moaning as she did so.*

*Instinctively she reached between his legs
and cupped his balls, massaging them as she
throated his cock as well as any professional
courtesan might have. Zane knew he was a goner,
but he couldn't do anything about it, so he just
threaded his hands into her silky blond hair and
pulsed deeply into her mouth, gratified as she
swallowed every last drop of his come.*

*He didn't know how long it was before he
was done shooting into the back of her throat, but
his legs were shaking. He didn't have the strength to
fight her, to show her who was boss, so he let her
pull him into the tub.*

He lay back against the rim and she straddled him and kissed him on his mouth, tasting his lips, playing with his tongue, nipping at his bottom lip.

"Jolene," he said, "I've got to tell you something."

Her face fell and her lips quivered slightly. He couldn't keep from laughing out loud.

Did she actually think for one minute that he'd break up with her?

Didn't she know he loved her more than life itself?

"Stop laughing at me!" She pounded his chest with her fists.

He grabbed her hands and held them still, saying, "What I wanted to tell you, you little fool, is that I'm in love with you."

Jolene grew completely still, then said, "Say that again?"

He reached for her face and pulled her down for a hard kiss. "I love you," he growled as he took her lips again.

Already hard again, he plunged his cock deep within her, taking immeasurable pleasure in filling her pussy with his shaft, in shooting his seed deep into her womb, in hearing her cry out his name.

Later, as she lay on his chest, with her head in the crook of his shoulder, she said, "I love you too, Zane," and he smiled and said, "Thank god," vowing to go to church again the next day, to give thanks for the woman in his arms.

Candace saved her file, quickly proofread it, and then printed it off for the contest. Sealing the envelope, she went to the post office and mailed it.

Knowing Charlie was waiting for her to come back to his house, she put the contest out of her mind, stuffed her deception and guilt away from her heart, and got in her car to drive straight to heaven.

* * * * *

The next three weeks were amazing. Candace and Charlie spent nearly all of their time together and had even begun to collaborate on an erotic novel together. Were it not for the black cloud of her dishonesty hanging over her head, she would have felt complete joy.

The problem was, every time she had an opportunity to tell him about her manuscript, she couldn't bring herself to do it. He was so damn good—so sweet and loving and tender—she hated the thought of ever seeing anything but love in his eyes.

Candace was desperately afraid he'd leave her if he found out how she betrayed the promise they'd made to each other. What had happened in their lessons was supposed to forever stay in their lessons, but by writing Jolene and Zane's tale she had broken that pledge.

As the days dragged by and she didn't hear a word from the contest judges, she began to irrationally hope that her entry had gotten lost in the mail. Or perhaps if she were lucky, the judges had hated it so much they just threw it away.

If Candace had it all to do over, if it meant preserving Charlie's love, she never would have written the manuscript.

Every day more of her clothes appeared in his closet. He wanted her to move in with him, but she told him it was too soon for such a big commitment.

A voice in her head said, *You would move in with him in a heartbeat if he knew what you had done and said he loved you anyway.*

Candace shook the voice off, and tried to stick to her story about needing more time. He was getting harder and harder to put off with each passing day, as they discovered depths of passion and love in each other's arms that neither had dreamed was even possible.

Her heart sank into her stomach as she saw the thick envelope waiting for her atop her pile of mail by the front door.

Feeling like she was suffocating, she picked up the envelope and sat down on the bottom step of her staircase. Sliding her finger underneath the seal, she slipped the papers out.

Dear Ms. Whitman, the cover letter read, *we are pleased to inform you that you are the Grand Prize Winner of the 15th Annual Erotic Writer's*

Contest! We hereby request your presence at the awards ceremony July 3rd. We are certain you will be thrilled to receive your medal and $10,000 check from our secret celebrity judge.

The paper fell through Candace's hands. "Oh my god," she whispered, "I won!"

She jumped up off of the step and screamed, "I won! I won!" and ran into the kitchen to call Charlie.

She stopped as everything crashed down around her. *She couldn't tell him.*

Tell him now, her rational inner-voice nagged her.

Unwilling to risk his love, Candace decided not to tell him about winning the award. And now she needed to think of a good excuse for why she was going to be busy on Saturday night.

"Damn it," she muttered as she went back into her foyer to pick up the contest papers that were strewn all over her hardwood floors and began to compose her newest lie in her head.

Chapter Thirteen

"Baby," Candace said as she lay in the crook of Charlie's arm, "I have a family thing this Saturday."

"Oh good. I've been dying to meet your family."

Inwardly she cursed herself for saying the wrong thing. "Actually," she said, "it's a private matter. I promise to tell you everything once things are ironed out, but for now, the lawyers have insisted we keep it within the family."

Charlie kissed the top of her head. "Sounds serious. Are you sure you don't want me to come along for moral support?"

"Definitely not!" she exclaimed. Realizing she had been far more fervent with her protests than was necessary, she stroked her hands through the golden hair that dusted his muscular chest. Trying to keep her tone light she said, "Hey, you'll finally get a day without me. I'll bet you've been dying to hang out with the guys to drink beer and eat pizza and watch sports, huh?"

Charlie chuckled. "Honestly? No. I haven't

been the least bit interested in hanging out with the guys."

"Really?" she asked in an uncertain voice.

"Are you kidding?" he replied. "Only a madman would choose beer and pizza over you."

She tilted her head up and kissed him softly on the lips. "I love you, Charlie Gibson."

* * * * *

Charlie had planned on asking Candace to the Erotic Writing Contest ceremony, but he kept forgetting. By the time he learned she already had unbreakable plans, he figured there was no point in mentioning it at all.

Backstage, in his dressing room, Charlie clipped on his bowtie and evened up the sleeves of his tux jacket. Looking at himself in the mirror he saw a man in love looking back at him. His eyes were clear and bright, a smile was permanently plastered on his face.

He was planning on asking her to marry him. In fact, he had dropped by Tiffany's that very afternoon. He couldn't wait to slip the solitaire on her finger, knowing she'd be in his bed, in his heart, for all eternity.

Steve Holt stuck his head in the door. "Hey Charlie, I thought you might want to check out the winning manuscript before you present the award to the winner." Steve put the thick bundle of pages on the table nearest the door. "It's pretty fuckin' hot. I can't wait to get a look at the woman who wrote it when she walks up on stage tonight."

Charlie cocked his head to the side. "You don't recognize the writer's name?"

"I think it's a pseudonym. Nobody would name their daughter Candy Lane."

Candy? Charlie felt a squeezing sensation in his chest, but brushed his sense of foreboding aside. Of course Candace hadn't turned herself into Candy Lane.

Then again, he had never asked her if she wrote under a pseudonym.

She would have told him if she entered this contest, he knew she would have. They told each other everything—all of their dreams, fears, hopes.

He shook his head to clear the insanity from it and picked up the manuscript. "Thanks Steve. I'll take a quick look at it. See you out there."

"I'll save you some champagne," Steve said and then loped off down the hall.

Charlie shut the door behind Steve, sat down on the leather sofa in the small dressing room and read, *"Jolene was a good girl..."*

* * * * *

Candace walked into the beautifully decorated ballroom of the Fairmont in Union Square and slid her hands over her red silk dress, smoothing out invisible wrinkles. She was incredibly nervous about accepting the award for her story, *Hell's Angel*. Yet again, she wished she had told Charlie about it, so he could lend her the moral support she so desperately needed.

A stunning blond greeted her at the doorway. "And you are?"

"Candace Whitman," Candace replied with a smile.

"Ooo, how exciting!" the woman exclaimed as she spontaneously gave Candace a hug. "Charlie Gibson was your mentor this year, wasn't he?"

Candace nodded. "That's right."

The woman leaned in closer and said, "Jessie was spitting nails for weeks after losing out on the chance to work with him. I hear you nabbed him the minute he walked into the conference hall."

Grinning, Candace said, "Pretty much," liking the woman immensely and feeling a great deal more at ease.

"I'm Sherryl Ann," the woman said with a shake of her perfect blond ringlets. "Charlie was my mentor last year and I learned so much from him. I'll bet you did too."

The smile froze on Candace's face. "You worked with Charlie last year?" she asked, striving for an even tone.

Sherryl Ann winked. "He's quite a hunk, isn't he?"

Candace felt all of the color rush out of her face just as a loud buzzing started in her ears. "He is," she said quickly. "Could you point me to the ladies room?"

"Sure thing, honey. It's just down the hall to the left. You don't look so good all of a sudden," the woman added, clearly concerned.

"Probably just something I ate," Candace lied before spinning around and practically running down the hall.

"I can't believe I'm such an idiot," she whispered. "Of course I wasn't the only female apprentice he's ever had." She sniffled and rolled some toilet paper into her fist, dashing it angrily at her face.

Painful memories crashed down around her. Walking in on her first boyfriend while he screwed the head cheerleader. Bravely letting her next boyfriend have sex with her, only to have him tell her she was a cold fish. Swallowing her pride as she found signs of her latest boyfriend's affair, and realizing it was with the woman she thought was her best friend.

And now Charlie. He had probably slept with every woman in the room on a "mentor/apprentice" basis.

She heaved in a shaky breath. "I'll show him," she declared. "I'm going to accept this award, shove it in his face, and move on with my life. Without him."

She unlatched the bathroom door and made her way to the mirror. Quickly fixing her makeup, she strode into the banquet hall and tried to ignore the voice in her heart that said she could never live without Charlie by her side.

* * * * *

The words played in endless repeat in Charlie's head and swam before his eyes.

"He hooked his fingers into the edges of her cotton panties and slowly slid them off her."

"Suddenly the buzzing started up again between her thighs, but this time, she knew that somehow, some way, Zane was manning the controls to her vagina."

" 'You're not wearing panties,' he said. 'I was wondering when you'd notice.' "

"I want you to soap me up."

Charlie ran his hands through his hair and dropped the manuscript back onto the table.

He had read the words, but he still couldn't believe it.

Candace had detailed their lessons act by act, scene by scene, in her book *Hell's Angel*. He couldn't deny that it was powerful writing, and yet the hole in his heart was so deep he could hardly feel anything at all.

"Damn it!" he exclaimed as he punched his hand into the wall. Some of the plaster crumbled beneath his fist just as the event organizer knocked once.

"What?" Charlie said in a gruff tone.

"We're ready for you," said the voice from the hall.

"I'll be right out."

He had thought he was special to Candace, but now he wondered if he was just a fool for believing that she truly loved him. For all he knew, she was going to take her new knowledge and find another "mentor", one who knew more than he did, who could give her things he couldn't.

Charlie took a deep breath and tried to compose himself. And then he stepped out of his dressing room, wondering what the hell he was going to say to her when they finally came face to face on stage.

* * * * *

The MC said, "Thank you for coming to the 15th Annual Erotic Writer's Contest awards ceremony! We had some incredible entries this year, but for the first time in the history of this contest, our judges voted unanimously for the winner. Here to present the $10,000 check to our winner is none other than best-selling author, Charlie Gibson."

Sitting out in the audience, Candace was hardly aware of the raucous hoots and hollers from the crowd. Charlie was the surprise celebrity guest?

She looked around for the nearest escape, but knew that she couldn't take the coward's way out. Not this time. Even if she ran tonight, he'd find out that Candy Lane was her pseudonym, that *Hell's Angel* had been inspired by their astonishing lovemaking.

It was finally time to face her fate.

Charlie took the stage and she could see him scanning the crowd, looking for her. His eyes locked with hers and she forced herself not to look away. She didn't know what she expected to see in his eyes—pain, hatred maybe—but not the awful blankness that radiated down to her in the audience.

Her stomach heaved, but she swallowed the bile back into her throat and clasped her hands tightly in her lap, her spine as straight as rebar.

"Writing is a funny thing," he began, as he looked out over the large, well-dressed crowd with a small smile. "We think that we can separate ourselves from the stories we weave, but no matter how much we lie to ourselves, there is always a piece of us in there. Some where, some way, we can never disguise what's in our heart."

"An hour ago Steve Holt handed me a copy of the winning manuscript. Truth is, folks, I couldn't put it down. It was compelling. It was sensual. And most of all, it was honest."

A tear slipped down Candace's cheek. "Stop, Charlie. Please, stop."

"It is with distinct pleasure that I award this year's Erotic Writer's award to Candace Whitman, for her erotic novel, *Hell's Angel*, writing as Candy Lane."

The applause was deafening as Candace unsteadily rose to her feet. Strangers reached out to shake her hand in congratulations. She smiled and murmured thanks, but she was held prisoner by the intensity of Charlie's gaze.

I love you and I'm sorry, her heart cried out to him, but by the look in his eyes, she knew he was lost to her.

Wiping away the tear that had rolled down her cheek, she carefully climbed the small flight of stairs up to the podium where Charlie was standing.

"I'm sorry," she mouthed to him, but he ignored her, his face devoid of all emotion.

Putting the check into her trembling hands, without touching her, he stepped back into the shadows. Fearing her knees were going to buckle beneath her, Candace clutched at the podium and held on for dear life.

Looking out at the rapt crowd who was waiting for her acceptance speech, she swallowed nervously.

"Hi," she said softly into the microphone, surprised by the volume of her voice through the speakers.

"I, uh, want to thank the judges for..." She cut herself off, shaking her head, her face crumpling. "The truth is, I can't accept this award. I'm sorry," she cried as a sob escaped her.

She ran off of the stage and down through the tables and chairs in the banquet room. She continued to run through the lobby and out into the cool evening air, not stopping to breathe until she tripped in her high heels and landed hard against a street lamp.

Clutching the street lamp, she gasped for air, hating herself more and more with every passing second.

She felt a warm hand on the small of her back through her thin silk dress.

"It's a wonderful book, Candy," Charlie said as he gently rubbed her back.

She shook her head so hard, her gold clip fell out of her hair and clattered to the sidewalk. "No. It's not. I'm sorry. I'm so sorry." She sniffled and wiped her nose with the back of her hand.

"Sweetheart," he said, his voice tender, "I love you."

She finally turned around to face him, anger mixing with her sorrow. "Is that what you told Sherryl Ann last year?"

"What does Sherryl Ann have to do with this?"

Candace crossed her cold hands across her chest and held onto her shoulders, rocking slightly back and forth as if to comfort herself.

"What kind of *lessons* did you set up for her? Were they hotter than ours?"

"God no! I edited a couple of her manuscripts and then passed her off to my agent."

Candace knew the look of shock and disbelief on Charlie's face was pure and she felt like an even bigger fool than before.

"I understand if you never want to see me again, Charlie," she said, staring at the dirty sidewalk between them.

He slipped one of his fingers underneath her chin and forced her to look him in the eye.

"Candy, I won't lie to you. This hurts like hell. I thought you knew you could tell me anything. Anything at all."

"I do," she protested, but he quieted her by pressing his thumb over her lips.

"The truth is I'll love you until the day I die, no matter what. So if you think I'm going to let the content of one of your future best-selling novels get in the way of our future, you're very much mistaken. It's gonna take a whole lot more than a few hot love scenes to change the way I feel about you, sweetheart."

New tears had formed in Candace's eyes, but this time they were tears of joy. She launched herself onto him, wrapping her long legs around his waist and kissed him with all of the love in her heart

"Oh baby," she said when they stopped devouring each other's lips for a moment, "I love you so much."

Charlie just smiled and held her closer to him, heedless of the stares from the strangers as they walked by.

"Thank god," he murmured as he bent his head and captured Candace's lips in a kiss that went straight to her soul.

"Now, let's get home so that I can punish you for your very bad behavior."

* * * * *

And so it was that Charlie finally got to enact the scene he had been choreographing in his imagination since the day he first lay Candace naked upon the bed in his guest bedroom and tasted her sweet pussy.

Charlie sat down on the edge of their bed, still wearing his tuxedo. "Come here," he said.

Candace couldn't hold back the smile on her lips as she walked towards him.

"What could you possibly be smiling about," he said, trying and failing to hold back his own grin, "when you are about to get spanked until your ass is pink and stinging?"

Candace made a show of demurely lowering her eyes, before looking up at him through her long lashes. "I am a very bad girl, and I deserve to be punished."

"Lie across my thighs," he ordered.

"What about my clothes?" she asked him, gesturing to her ankle-length red silk dress.

"Leave your clothes to me. Now get over here."

Hiding another smile, but unable to disguise the twinkle in her eyes, Candace draped her body, face down, across the tops of Charlie's thighs.

Through the smooth, thin silk of her dress, he rubbed her round, firm ass.

"No panties?" he asked hoarsely.

In a subservient voice she said, "I wouldn't dare wear panties. Not when you're already about to discipline me."

"Good girl," he said, licking his lips.

Unexpectedly, he ripped the seam of Candace's dress open from her ankle to her waist. She gasped and he said, "See how upset I am with you?"

She nodded and waited expectantly for his onslaught to begin. Already, her pussy was moist and swollen, ready to be touched, sucked, and fucked.

Again, he rubbed the palm of his right hand on her bottom, warming up her chilled flesh.

"You have such a beautiful ass," he murmured. He lifted up his hand and then brought it down firmly.

Candace gasped again as pleasure and pain got all mingled up inside of her.

"Am I hurting you?" Charlie asked her, his voice hot with need.

"A little," she said in a small voice, equally wracked with the need to be possessed by the man she loved.

He ran his hand down her ass cheek to the very top of her thighs and then slid an index finger inside her swollen pussy. "What about now?" he asked, his breath coming in quick bursts. "Am I hurting you now?"

"You could never hurt me."

Abruptly, Charlie ripped the dress all the way up to her shoulders. She was completely naked underneath and he lowered her to the soft rug in front of his bed. She looked up at him with love in her eyes.

"Now for the final punishment," he said, as he unzipped his pants and let his huge, throbbing shaft spring free. Settling himself between her legs, he pushed into her wet, hot pussy, inch by inch.

"Charlie," she moaned, her head writhing on the floor.

"Oh god," he roared as she moved her hips slightly, taking him all the way to the hilt. Roughly he grabbed her hips, feeling her muscles contract around him as her pleasure spiraled out of control.

Right before they came, Charlie forced their bodies to go completely still. Holding her hips in his hands, he watched the rise and fall of her breasts as she panted beneath him.

"I love you Candy. Don't you ever forget it again."

And then he plunged into her hot folds, and she milked him dry as a soul-shattering orgasm rocked through them both.

The next day, they wrote their latest lovemaking into their new tale of erotic romance and then headed back to the bedroom for another round of "research."

~ THE END ~